CHARLEMAGNE
AND THE PALADINS

BY JULIA CRESSWELL
ILLUSTRATED BY MIGUEL COIMBRA

First published in Great Britain in 2014 by Osprey Publishing,
Kemp House, Chawley Park, Cumnor Hill, Oxford, OX2 9PH, UK
4301 21st. St., Suite 220, Long Island City, NY 11101, USA
E-mail: info@ospreypublishing.com

Osprey Publishing is part of the Osprey Group

A CIP catalog record for this book is available from the British Library

Print ISBN: 978 1 4728 0416 7
PDF e-book ISBN: 978 1 4728 0418 1
EPUB e-book ISBN: 978 1 4728 0417 4

Typeset in Garamond Pro and Myriad Pro

Originated by PDQ Media, Bungay, UK
Printed in China through Asia Pacific Offset Limited

14 15 16 17 18 10 9 8 7 6 5 4 3 2 1

Osprey Publishing is supporting the Woodland Trust, the UK's leading woodland conservation
charity, by funding the dedication of trees.

www.ospreypublishing.com

CONTENTS

INTRODUCTION   4

CHARLEMAGNE IN HISTORY AND LEGEND   6
Bertha Bigfoot ❧ Charlemagne's Ancestors ❧ Describing the Historical
Charlemagne ❧ Describing the Fictional Charlemagne ❧ The Young
Charlemagne ❧ Charlemagne's Adventures in Jerusalem and Constantinople ❧
Charlemagne and Harun al-Rashid ❧ Charlemagne the Sinner

THE PALADINS   17
The Major Paladins ❧ Other Key Characters

THE SONG OF ROLAND   23
An Embassy from Marsile ❧ The Betrayal ❧ The Pass of Roncevalles ❧
The Second Assault ❧ The Death of Roland ❧ Charlemagne's Dream ❧
The Final Battle ❧ Trial by Combat

ROLAND AND OLIVER   35
The First Meeting ❧ Fierabras the Giant ❧ The Giant Ferragus

GUY OF BURGUNDY   41

OGIER THE DANE   46
Ogier the Outlaw ❧ The Later Tales of Ogier

TURPIN   53
The Pseudo-Turpin

THE ITALIAN VERSIONS   58
Orlando Innamorato ❧ Rogero and Bradamante ❧ Orlando Furioso

CHILDE ROLAND   67

CHARLEMAGNE'S LONG AFTERLIFE   72
Charlemagne's Tomb ❧ Sainthood and Politics

FURTHUR READING   79

INTRODUCTION

There was once a time, not too long ago, that stories about Charlemagne were as well-known as those about King Arthur. Why they have fallen out of fashion is a puzzle, because they are just as varied, interesting and exciting as those about Arthur and his knights. Perhaps we are uncomfortable because Charlemagne is a historical figure, and we dislike mixing fact and fiction. For many centuries the stories in this book were treated as historical fact. It was only in the 18th century that people began to seriously question the story presented by the legends. There are many inconsistencies and downright contradictions in the stories, and people must have begun to suspect that miracles did not happen quite as conveniently in real life as they did for Charlemagne in the legends.

There are over a thousand stories about Charlemagne and his paladins told in almost every Western European language, from Welsh, Irish, and Icelandic to Basque, French, and Latin. The greatest number is in German and, of course, French. The same basic stories were shared in many of the languages, but with each re-telling details and emphasis would change, subject to the creativity of the teller, so that a story at one end of the chain could differ considerably from that at the other. This process gives us an idea of how the stories developed. There is a core of truth underneath the main stories, which may be another reason that it took so long to disentangle fact and fiction. This process has been called 'mythistory', where fact and fiction feed into each other. A similar process can be seen at work in modern times, where stories of cowboys in the American West or of fighting in World War II, in both print and film, often blend fact and fiction. In the case of Charlemagne and his paladins, the stories arose in a time when written sources were not readily available, and episodes associated with one person could easily be confused with those that happened to another. This was particularly the case with Charlemagne's successors.

Charlemagne's great empire started to crumble soon after his death in AD 814. His only surviving son, Louis the Pious (also known as Louis the Feeble), was deposed and restored several times by his own sons. The empire was split into three under Louis's sons and had disintegrated into many kingdoms by the next generation. The lands Charlemagne had once ruled were riven by civil war and invasions by Vikings from the north and west and Magyars from the east. Both groups of invaders reached Paris in the course of the 9th century. Charlemagne's successors included another Louis, Louis the German, and two more named Charles – Charles the Bald, a grandson of the great Charles (the meaning of the name Charlemagne), and Charles the Fat, who was a great-grandson, but only a few years younger than Charles the Bald. Their nicknames give a pretty good impression of how they were regarded as rulers.

Events that happened under these successor rulers got muddled up in popular imagination with those of Charlemagne's and of his predecessors' reigns. During this time of chaos, which lasted for some 200 years, people looked back on Charlemagne's time as a golden age of peace and prosperity, adding yet another element to the tendency to turn fact into fiction.

There is some evidence that full-length narratives about Charlemagne and his paladins were circulating in the 9th century, and they were certainly being told in the 10th century. It is these stories that make up a large proportion of the medieval writings known as the 'Matter of France', and which are the focus of this book.

A reconstruction of the historical Charlemagne by Angus McBride. (Osprey Publishing)

CHARLEMAGNE IN HISTORY AND LEGEND

Charlemagne so dominated his age, and his real life contained so many episodes that could come from the imagination of a storyteller, that historians still have a hard job separating fact from fiction. Fictional stories about him were circulating while those who had known him were still alive and had probably appeared before his death, in his early seventies, in January 814.

We do not know exactly when Charlemagne was born, although it must have been around 742, nor where, although in the past much energy was expended by nationalistic writers in France and Germany trying to prove that it was in their country – a singularly futile exercise, as there is no evidence one way or the other. Charlemagne was born into a family of distinguished warriors. His grandfather was Charles Martel, the nickname Martel referring both to his resemblance to the Roman god of war Mars and the Old French word for 'the hammer'. He had indeed hammered the raiding Muslims at the battle of Poitiers in 732 after they invaded from their newly acquired base in Spain. Charles Martel was not king of the Franks, but had the title Mayor of the Palace, which meant that he was effectively ruler on behalf of the last Merovingian kings, whose role was now merely symbolic. Charles' two sons, Pepin the Short and Carloman, inherited power from their father, and after Carloman retired into a monastery Pepin was left in sole power. In 751 Pepin had himself declared king and made his son Charles, later known as Charlemagne, his heir.

Bertha Bigfoot

Charlemagne's mother was Bertrada (whose name also appears as Bertrade, Bertha and Bert(h)e). As the daughter of Count Charibert of Laon, she came from a very influential family. At this time, marriage was regarded as a matter of private contract and not a church matter. Charlemagne himself was to make and break a number of marriages and had a number of concubines.

At the time of Charlemagne's birth, Bertrada had a role that might be called a 'recognized companion' although Pepin made her his official queen shortly thereafter. The real Bertrada lived a long life, dying in 782, and had an influential role in Charlemagne's early years as a ruler. In legend, however, she was to live even longer and lead an even more exciting life. There she is known as Bertha Bigfoot, the daughter of Floris and Blanchefleur, a couple who have their own long romance in medieval stories. Over 20 versions of Bertha's story survive from the Middle Ages alone, so there are many variations, but the oldest versions say that Bertha was so famous for her beauty that Pepin, king of France, asked to marry her, and her parents agreed to send her to him from Hungary, where they were king and queen. She travelled with her old nurse Margiste and her daughter Alise, who looked remarkably like Bertha. On the wedding night, Margiste had Bertha abducted by assassins, and Alise took Bertha's place in the wedding bed. The assassins, however, could not bring themselves to kill Bertha, so they left her to wander in a forest, where she would have died from hunger and exposure if she had not been rescued by Pepin's cowherd Symon and his wife Constance.

A statue of Charlemagne's mother, Bertha, in the Luxembourg Gardens, Paris. (Serge Angeric / Alamy)

Bertha refused to reveal her true identity and became Symon's servant, while Alise took her name and role as queen. Alise was so detested because of her bad temper and arrogant behaviour that Blanchefleur travelled to France to see what had gone wrong, for her daughter had never behaved badly in the past. When Blanchefleur arrived, Alise pretended to be ill and hid under the bedcovers in a darkened room, hoping to escape detection. However, her feet stuck out from the bed covers, and Blanchefleur realized that they were far too small to be her daughter's. Thus the plot was revealed and the perpetrators hanged.

Pepin was left without a wife, for there was no news of Bertha. But then one day he went hunting in the forest. Versions differ as to how he and Bertha were reunited. The politest version says that she rescued him from a wild boar that attacked him. Another version says that she revealed who she was when Pepin tried to rape her. The oldest surviving version, which is probably closest to what life was really like for the underclass at the time, says that Symon simply gave his servant to Pepin to sleep with. This version also says that a bed was made up on a cart for them, and there Charlemagne was conceived. This is typical medieval word-play, for the Latin for a cart, *carrus*, resembles the Latin form of Charles, *Carolus,* while the French for cart, *char*, also looks like Charles.

Charlemagne's Ancestors

This cart story is nonsense, but Charlemagne's name did carry a wealth of meaning. Names were very important in the Frankish ruling families. Charlemagne was given the name of his grandfather, Charles Martel, which meant that he was expected to be a great soldier. The name 'Charles' means

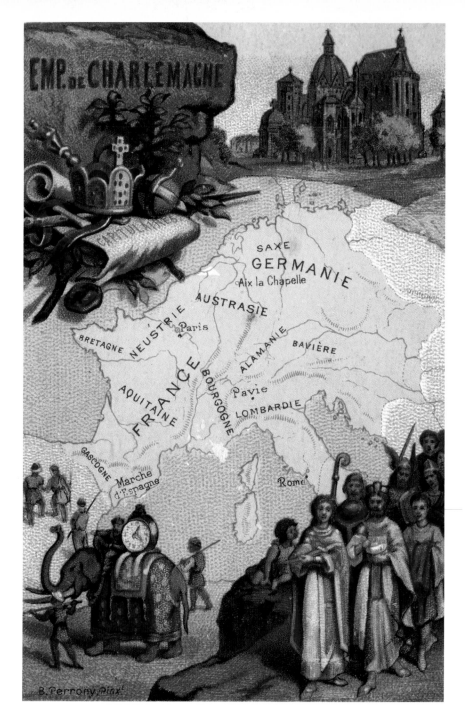

something like 'manly', and Charlemagne's life showed a pattern of energy and enterprise that the name seemed to predict. He would have grown up feeling chosen for success. It was not just that he was the eldest son of a king, and had been anointed by the pope himself as his father's successor. The Franks thought of themselves as the chosen people of their time and saw themselves the natural replacement for the now degenerate Romans. Charlemagne's family knew it was even more special. Paul the Deacon, a member of Charlemagne's court, wrote of hearing Charlemagne himself tell the story behind this. His family was descended from St Arnulf, bishop of Metz (*c.*582–640). Arnulf, Charlemagne claimed, threw a precious ring into the River Moselle, as a penance for his sins, saying that he would only regard himself as forgiven if the ring was returned to him. Some years later his cook found the ring in the stomach of a fish he was preparing to serve the bishop, and this miracle showed the bishop was forgiven. This is a well-known and ancient international folktale, found in the writings of Herodotus in the 5th century BC, but there is nothing to suggest that Charlemagne did not believe it was true of his ancestor.

A silver coin with a head of Charlemagne. This is our best evidence for what he looked like. (Mary Evans)

Describing the Historical Charlemagne

Einhard, who had worked for Charlemagne, gives a description of the man he knew in the *Life of Charlemagne* he wrote after he retired from court life. Although he modelled his description on ones from classical Latin literature, this does not mean that it is not accurate. He describes Charlemagne as heavily built and taller than average, around 6ft 3in. He had a round head, bright eyes and white hair in old age. He had a short fat neck and a bit of a potbelly. Einhard mentions his love of roast meat, so by implication the two are connected. He had a rather high-pitched voice for one of his build and remained fit and vigorous into old age. His coins show him with the traditional Frankish short hair, shaved chin and long moustache.

Charlemagne also took pride in dressing in the traditional costume of the Franks and habitually wore a belted knee-length tunic over trousers, caught below the knee by strips of cloth tightly bound round the calves down to the feet. He wore a blue cloak and an otter or sheepskin jerkin in cold weather. He always wore a sword, silver hilted for everyday use, gold for special days, when he might also wear richer tunics. He is reputed to have been critical of fashion-victims, commenting that the fashion for short cloaks meant that you froze your backside when you had to go outside to relieve yourself.

Charlemagne was something of a control freak when it came to governing his empire and his family, refusing to let any of his daughters marry. Instead he kept them with him at court, an unusual attitude in an age where the main role of daughters was to make useful marriage alliances.

His favourite recreation was swimming in the natural hot springs of his capital of Aachen (known in French as Aix-la-Chapelle). Alcuin of York, the Englishman who served Charlemagne for many years and who played such a major role in the remarkable revival of learning under him, has left us an account of having to join him in the pool in order to discuss theology, and elsewhere we hear that he sometimes invited all his guards to join him, so that more than 100 men would be swimming together.

THE SCHOOL OF THE PALACE

Charlemagne was much
admired in the 19th century
as a supporter of education.
Marion Florence Lansing's
Barbarian and Noble (1911),
imagines him visiting Alcuin
as he teaches.

Charlemagne was much
admired in the 19th century
as a supporter of education.
Marion Florence Lansing's
Barbarian and Noble (1911),
imagines him visiting Alcuin
as he teaches.

Describing the Fictional Charlemagne

The Charlemagne of fiction has a very different appearance. He is old – over 200 in *The Song of Roland* – and has long white hair and an even longer white beard. There are various reasons for this image. The historical Charlemagne did live to be quite old. As he had come to the throne in 768 and reigned for 46 years, for the majority of his subjects he was the only ruler they had known. He was such a dominant figure in his time that in the popular mind the deeds of his predecessors and heirs became blurred with his reign, making it seem even longer. But the main reason for his age was his role as the champion of Christendom. Taking their cue from the Old Testament, medieval authors easily imagined that someone so favoured by God would live longer than average. In *The Song of Roland* and other texts, he can be shown as bowed down by age, but at other times his appearance can be imposing.

In the *Pseudo-Turpin Chronicle*, he is described as dark-haired, well proportioned, handsome and 8ft tall. His face was a palm and a half in length, his beard a palm. He had the eyes of a lion and could instill terror into any who opposed his will. His girdle was eight palms long, not counting the part that hung loose. He ate little bread but could consume a quarter of a sheep, or two chickens, or a goose, or a leg of pork, or a peacock, or a crane, or a whole hare, at one meal. He drank little wine. He was also immensely strong. With one blow of his sword he could split an armed and mounted knight and his horse together. He could easily bend four horseshoes at once, and he could stand a knight in armour on his palm and lift him as high as his head.

The Young Charlemagne

Although he generally appears in the stories as old, we are given some information about his fictional life as a young man. One story tells us that as a youth Charlemagne escaped from his dishonourable guardians (some say the sons Pepin had by the false Bertha) and fled to Spain, where he took service with Galafre, emir of Toledo, under the pseudonym of Mainet. There he distinguished himself so much that the emir offered him his daughter in marriage and to make him his heir. Charlemagne refused the kingdom, but accepted the daughter, Galienne, after she agreed to convert to Christianity.

Another story deals with events leading up to the coronation of Charlemagne, and is told as an example of God's favour to him. His sleep was disturbed one night by a vision of an angel, telling him to go out and steal. Feeling it was ridiculous for a king to be a thief, Charlemagne rolled over

This little bronze statue in the Louvre is traditionally said to be a portrait of Charlemagne. It was probably made too late to be taken from life, but may be an idealised portrait of Charlemagne made in the reign of his grandson Charles the Bald. (Ancient Art & Architecture Collection Ltd / Alamy)

and went back to sleep, only to receive the divine message a second time. So he got up, dressed suitably, picked up his sword, and crept out into the night. In the woods Charlemagne met a man he had exiled and who had become a notorious robber. Charlemagne tried to persuade him to go with him to rob the court, but the robber refused to act against his king. Instead, he suggested robbing a local nobleman. The two crept into his house and overheard the nobleman telling his wife about the plot he and his allies had made to dethrone Charlemagne. Armed with this information, Charlemagne was able to arrest the conspirators and secure his throne. The robber was rewarded by forgiveness and promotion. In the French versions of the story the robber is called Basin, but in the Germanic traditions he is Elegast or Elbegast, a name that means 'elf-spirit' and which is associated with the king of the elves. The events of the story are said to have taken place at Ingelheim, a town on the Rhine, whose name means 'angel's home', referring to the angelic visions of Charlemagne.

Charlemagne's Adventures in Jerusalem and Constantinople

There are many stories of Charlemagne's dealings with the Holy Land, many of which contain little fact and a great deal of fiction. Among them is a peculiar Old French poem called *The Pilgrimage of Charlemagne to Jerusalem and Constantinople*, which has puzzled generations of scholars with its apparent mixture of seriousness and satire. The story starts with Charlemagne and his wife quarrelling because she suggests that the emperor of Constantinople holds higher state than Charlemagne. Furious, the king decides that he and his peers will set off on pilgrimage to Jerusalem, taking in Constantinople on the way back. They duly arrive at Jerusalem, enter the great church and seat themselves on the chairs used for the Last Supper – Charlemagne on Jesus' chair and the peers on the chairs of the apostles. The patriarch of Jerusalem is summoned by a passing native, who asks to be converted because he thinks that Jesus and the apostles have returned.

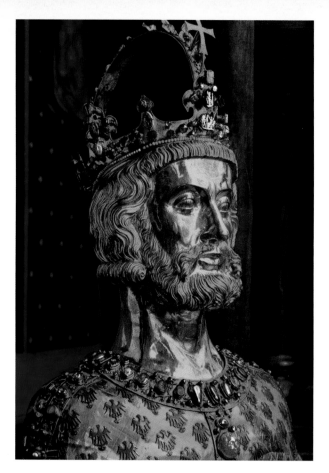

This reliquary bust of Charlemagne, containing a piece of his skull, it was made *c.*1349, and the detachable crown may sometimes have been used in Imperial coronation ceremonies. Aachen Cathedral Treasury. (INTERFOTO / Alamy)

The patriarch was impressed by Charles and his knights, and declared that Charles should henceforth be called Charlemagne, Charles the Great, and proclaimed him emperor. He also handed over a number of holy relics that Charlemagne took back with him to the abbey of St Denis near Paris. The party then went to Constantinople, which was indeed glorious and rich, and became guests of the emperor Hugo (no such emperor ever existed). They were housed in a room of overwhelming magnificence, but Hugo left a spy hidden there. The Franks got drunk and began a boasting game, each trying to outdo the other in their outrageous boasts. Turpin would ride three horses at once while juggling four apples. Garin would throw a spear at two pennies placed on a tower half a league away and knock one off without touching the other, then run so quickly that he would catch the spear before it touched the ground. Berenger would jump from the highest tower on to the points of swords set up at its base without being wounded. Bertram would fly like a bird using two shields for wings. Ogier would pull down the central pillar of the palace. Oliver would make love to the emperor's beautiful daughter 100 times in one night.

When these boasts were reported to Hugo he was furious, and despite Charlemagne explaining that it was all drunken fun and never meant to be taken seriously, Hugo insisted that the paladins perform these deeds or have their heads cut off. There was nothing for it but to get the holy relics they had brought with them from Jerusalem and to pray hard. The archangel Gabriel was sent to answer their prayers and said they would have divine support for their deeds, but to be more careful in the future. As a result they all succeeded, except for Oliver, who only managed 30 times, but the emperor's daughter was so impressed that she fibbed to her father that he had fulfilled his vow. (Galien, the son resulting from this night of passion, gets to have a whole cycle of stories of his own.) Hugo admits Charlemagne's superiority, and when in the ensuing revels the two emperors are compared, it is seen that Charlemagne is considerably taller than Hugo, and concluded that he literally holds higher state. Thus honour is satisfied.

Charlemagne and Harun al-Rashid

More serious pseudo-chronicles claim that Charlemagne conquered the Holy Land, and while he in fact never got anywhere near Jerusalem, there is evidence to support the claim that in the year 800, after Charlemagne's coronation as western emperor by the pope, the patriarch of Jerusalem did symbolically send him the keys of the Holy Sepulchre and gave him the title of Protector of the Holy Places. This indicated that the patriarch now regarded Charlemagne, rather than the Byzantine emperor, as the protector of the Christians there. In fact, in one of those moments in which truth is stranger than fiction, the historical Charlemagne had cordial relations with Harun al-Rashid, the caliph of Baghdad, a man, as any reader of the *Thousand and One Nights* will know, mythologized just as much as Charlemagne.

The coronation sword of the kings of France, supposedly Charlemagne's Joyeuse. Its true date is disputed, but parts, particularly the pommel, may date from the time of Charlemagne. It was used as part of the regalia for the kings of France into the 19th century and is now in the Louvre. (The Art Gallery Collection / Alamy)

The two exchanged gifts. Charlemagne sent hounds, horses and precious fabrics. Harun sent wonders from the East: silks, spices, a magnificent pavilion, monkeys, candelabras. He sent mechanical wonders lost to the West such as an organ and a magnificent brass water clock that on the hour dropped a weight that rang a cymbal while twelve model horsemen moved round. Above all, he sent an elephant.

Isaac the Jew (whose name reminds us how much more cosmopolitan society at the time was than is often imagined) had been sent four years earlier as Charlemagne's ambassador to Harun. He had walked the elephant some three and a half thousand miles from Baghdad to Aachen, crossed the sea from North Africa to Italy, and had arrived at Aachen in 802. The elephant created a sensation. It is frequently mentioned in writings of the time, and we even know its name, Abul-Abbas. In fact, we know more about the elephant than we do about many important men of the time – the real-life person behind the paladin Roland, for example.

Abul Abbas, the elephant sent to Charlemagne by the Caliph Harun al-Rashid, is presented to the emperor and his court.

Dicuil, an Irish monk and scholar at Charlemagne's court, refers to Abul-Abbas as evidence to refute the claims of Roman writers that elephants cannot lie down. They lie, he says, 'for they lie down like an ox, as all the people of the Franks saw in the time of the Emperor Charles' (not that this stopped people repeating the error for many hundreds of years). The elephant has developed his own mythology. He is often described as a white elephant, and even quite reputable historians give descriptions of his leading processions or troops, for neither of which is there any contemporary evidence. However, we do know that Charles took Abul-Abbas with him when he crossed the Rhine to muster troops against the Danes in 810, for the *Frankish Annals* record the animal's death. The area where this is thought to have happened is rich in mammoth fossils, and finds of large bones were being identified as Abul-Abbas' remains into the 18th century.

Charlemagne the Sinner

Legend does not always show Charlemagne as a magnificent emperor. He is often shown as weak and unjust to his lords, particularly when dealing with the transgressions of his sons. One of the earliest stories to show him in a bad light comes from a 9th century *Life of St Giles*, which tells of an unspecified 'King Charles' who had committed a sin so great that he did not dare confess it. St Giles was miraculously able to get him absolution for this sin. Although this story was originally meant to glorify Giles, human nature being what it is, people were keen to know what this sin was.

Two different traditions developed. In France the sin became incest with Charlemagne's sister, with Roland as their child. In Germany, the sin was necrophilia. The story developed that Charlemagne's mistress had ensnared his love with a magic ring. When she was dying, she asked her maids to place it under her tongue. The body was prepared for burial, but the magic worked on, and Charlemagne would not let her be buried or leave her alone. A wise knight (or else St Giles) guessed what had happened, and removed the ring. Without the magic, Charlemagne was disgusted by the decaying corpse. Unfortunately, one version says, the magic still worked, and Charlemagne transferred his attention to the knight, who, to escape his attentions, threw the ring into a local marsh.

The continued power of the ring meant that Charles chose this place, later called Aachen, for his great palace, and it was why he liked to spend so much time swimming in the hot springs.

Signature of Charlemagne. The monogram is formed from the letters KAROLUS, the Latin form of his name.

THE PALADINS

We are used to the word 'paladin' meaning a mighty warrior, but historically Charlemagne's paladins were simply members of his court. The word comes from the same root as 'palace'. However, since Charlemagne was always on the move, 'paladin' referred to a person's function, rather than the resident of one place. Charlemagne's original paladins had posts such as that of constable (i.e. count of the stable) responsible for the supply of horses to the court and the army; chamberlain, responsible for state finances; count palatine, who was the most senior appeals judge; and seneschal, responsible for the many crown properties. However, these men were also warriors. The seneschal Eggihard and the count palatine Anselm fell at Roncevalles alongside Roland, while the chamberlain Adalgisile and the constable Geilo fell at the battle of Süntel in 782. But by at least the 11th century 'paladin' was being used as a term for a mighty fighter.

In fiction the number of Charlemagne's paladins was traditionally set at 12, and 'douzepers', from the French for '12 peers', was an alternative term for them. In fact, there were always more than 12 of them, as many medieval writers commented. The traditional number was symbolic. As champions of Christianity, they matched the number of Christ and his apostles, appropriate for an emperor who could be seen as Christ's representative on earth. The reason the numbers increased was for narrative purposes. In the same way as the writers of a long-running television series need to have a steady turnover of characters, the writers of the great medieval cycles of stories had to have a varied cast. Some got killed, for reasons of verisimilitude or drama, or the audience got bored with hearing about one hero and craved the excitement of new characters. Moreover, in the Charlemagne stories, most of the paladins are very loosely based on real-life personages, usually from rather later in history, although in the case of Anseis much earlier. Writers would have to fit their plots to a particular audience who would want their local hero to appear. Add to this the fact that we are dealing with the works of many different authors, writing over several centuries, and it is no wonder that there is little overall consistency in the cycle of stories.

The Four Sons of Aymon, led by Reynard with his horse Bayard who could carry all four of them, depicted in a 15th century manuscript. (Bridgeman Art Library)

The Major Paladins

Here is a list of the most common paladins, with a brief description of who they were, and the most significant facts about them, taken from various sources. Of the many possible forms of their names, those used in *The Song of Roland* or the standard English forms of their names have been given preference.

In our key text, *The Song of Roland*, Charlemagne has the following paladins, who together with Roland and Oliver make 12. All die at the battle of Roncevalles. Each paladin had a sworn companion as brother in arms, the sort of relationship we are familiar with from the buddy movie. For convenience, they are described in their pairs, when the companion is known.

Charlemagne

Also known as Charles, Charles the Great, Karolus Magnus (Latin), Karl der Grosse (German). His sword was called Joyeuse ('Joyous') because of the holy relics that were mounted in its hilt. His horse was Tencendur ('Strife') or occasionally Blanchard ('Whitey'). His war cry was 'Mountjoy', the name of the mountain northwest of Jerusalem from which a pilgrim could get his first sight of Jerusalem. His battle standard was the Oriflamme ('gold flame') because it displayed gold flames on a red background.

Roland

Also known as Rolland, Rollant, Rodlan or Rolando in Spanish and Orlando in Italian. He carries the sword Durendal. His horn is called Oliphant ('elephant [ivory]'), and his horse is named Veillantif ('watchful, alert'). His companion is Oliver. He is the nephew of Charlemagne, his mother being Charlemagne's sister, given various names. Charlemagne's only sister in real life was called Gisela. Roland's father is either Milo or else Charlemagne, and his stepfather Ganelon.

Some sources give him a son, Baudoin. Sometimes this is the name of his brother, sometimes it is Ganelon's son. Historically, Roland was count of the Breton Marches, but some stories call him count of Le Mans and prince of Blaye, others earl of Cenonia. His shield is often shown in art with a lion rampant, usually red on a yellow background, although sometimes he is shown with other heraldry, such as the fleur de lis. At the time of his death he was betrothed to Aude, Oliver's sister.

Oliver

Also known as Olivier, companion to Roland. His sword is Hauteclere ('high bright, very bright') and after he captured him from the Saracen giant, Fierabras, he rode the horse, Ferrant, probably best translated as 'goer', although the meaning is sometimes given as 'traveller'. In art his shield sometimes bears the device of a maiden. He is count of Geneva. His father is Renier of Gennes, lord of the Val de Runers. Some call him a cousin to Roland. His sister is the beautiful Aude, betrothed to Roland. He has a squire called Garin, and sometimes two sons, Griffon and Aquilant, as well as Galien by the daughter of the emperor of Byzantium. While Roland is known for his bravery, Oliver is known for his level-headed wisdom.

Anseis
Known for his fierceness, his historical prototype may have been Ansegilis, father of Pepin II (who was father of Charles Martel, Charlemagne's grandfather), who died before 679, but whose name lived on. In *Anseis of Carthage* he is supposed to have survived Roncevalles and had further adventures. His companion was **Samson**, who is duke of Burgundy in some texts. His name also appears as Sampson, Sanson or Sansun, and in Italian texts he is Sansonetto.

Berenger
His name appears in this form in *The Song of Roland*, but in many other forms elsewhere including Bryer(e), Berard and, in Italian, Berlinghieri. He is lord of Montdidier. His companion is **Otes** or Oton.

Engler of Gascony
Also called Engelers or Engellers, we know little about him other than that he was brave and came from Bordeaux. We are not told his companion, and he appears in few stories outside the *Song*. He may be based on Angilbert (d. 814), diplomat, poet, courtier, and saint, despite the fact that he had two illegitimate children by one of Charlemagne's daughters. He later mutated into St Engelbert, famous for his magic powers.

Gerard of Rousillon
Also appearing as Girard, Gherard, Gerart, Girard, and Girart, in *The Song of Roland* he is usually called 'Gerard the Old'. There is also a 'Gerard of Montdidier' who appears in some texts. Gerard is also the hero of his own cycle of stories, sometimes as Girart of Vienne, where he appears as a rebel against the throne, and has a wife called Bertha. His real-life original was a Burgundian noble who lived in the 9th century and became count of Paris in 837. Like his fictional character, he founded several monasteries.

Gerer
We know little about Gerer other than that his horse was called Passecerf ('Stag-beater', i.e. faster than a stag). His companion was **Gerin**, lord of Vienne. His horse was called Sorel and he carried a red shield.

Ivon and Ivoire
Although they appear regularly in the stories, little is known about these two companions. Their names also appear as Ive, Yvon and Yvoire. It has been suggested that Yvon may derive from Eudon of Aquitaine who died in 735.

Other Key Characters

Naimes

Also known as Naymes, Naimon, Namo, and many other variants. He is duke of Bavaria. Much older than most of the other characters, he is a wise and experienced councillor, Charlemagne's chief adviser. He is one of the most frequently appearing characters in the stories.

Turpin

Archbishop of Reims, and a great fighter. His sword is called Almace, possibly 'the cutter' from Arabic. He survives at Roncevalles right to the end, dying while trying to get water for the wounded Roland. Some said he did indeed survive the battle, writing the definitive history of events.

Ogier

Although Ogier the Dane appears as a baron of Charlemagne's in *The Song of Roland*, he is not listed there as a peer, although he is usually listed among them in other works. His sword is Cortana ('the short' from its broken tip) and his horse is Broiefort (a name which has several possible translations, 'hard pounder' from the animal's endurance, or perhaps 'strong test' from the difficulty of taming it, or 'hard smasher' from its fierceness). He has his own chapter later in this book.

Ganelon

Although he is the perennial villain in the stories, there is no doubt that Ganelon is a fine warrior and skilful advisor. His fault is that he puts his personal pride and honour above that of the realm and his king. He also seems to have the misfortune not to fit in with the pervading attitude of Roland and his like of 'if in doubt, hit them'. He has a much more subtle and complex approach to life. Although he is generally known as Ganelon, this may be a pet form, possibly condescending, of the other form of his name, Guenes. He is also called Gan, Gano, and many other forms such as Guenelun and Guenelyn. His sword is called Murgleys, Murgleis or Murglies. This is sometimes interpreted as meaning 'death sword', or from the Arabic for 'valiant piercer'. His horse is Tachebrun ('brown spot'). His father was Griffon d'Hauteville, himself a son of Doon de Mayence (i.e. Mainz), who has his own cycle of stories, and is the grandfather of most of Charlemagne's rebellious barons.

Ganelon has a large extended family that supports him. His son, Baudoin or Baldwin, in some versions turns up at the last minute at Roncevalles and dies fighting with the rest of the rearguard. Ganelon is widely regarded as getting his name from the historical Wanilo, archbishop of Sens, who was accused in 859 by Charles the Bold, king of the Franks, of having betrayed him for money to Louis the German, a rival grandson of Charlemagne.

Golden Psalter of St Gall, a manuscript of *c*.750 showing how Charlemagne's cavalry might really have appeared. (The Art Archive / Alamy)

THE LATER PALADINS

The following is a select list of some of the warriors who appear as paladins in later stories.

Aymon

Also known as Aymeri or Aymer of Narbonne or Dordone, he was father of the more famous Reynard, and is sometimes said to have owned the sword Flamberge and the horse Bayard before his son. He is Charlemagne's brother-in-law, having married his sister Aya. When his sons rebel, he is torn between two loyalties. Aymon shares a vow with the historical 9th century Hadhemar, count of Narbonne, not to sleep under a roof during the war against the Saracens.

Bertrand

He appears as a paladin in the earliest surviving Latin fragment of the Charlemagne legend. In this very early text, which dates from the 10th or early 11th century, but which seems to have been a translation of a French text written a century earlier, Bertrand, Ernaut and Guibelin are the sons of Aymon of Narbonne's brothers, and therefore cousins to Reynard. These warriors are more prominent in the stories about Garin than those about Charlemagne.

Constantine

Prefect of Rome, he was killed at Roncevalles and buried in the Alyscamps cemetery in Arles, France.

Guy of Burgundy

Cousin of Charlemagne, and defender of Rome, he receives his own chapter later in this book.

Hoel

He was the Breton earl or count of Nantes.

Reynard

Also known as Renaude, Reinold, Raynold, Renau(l)t, Renaud, Reinold, and, in Italian, Rinaldo, lord of Montauban ('white mount'). His sword, Floberge or Flamberge, may be made by Wayland the Smith or belong in a set with Durendal. His horse, Bayard ('bay coloured'), is fast, strong and super-intelligent, and when Reynard and his brothers are in conflict with their lord, Bayard easily carries them all to safety. They take refuge from Charlemagne in the Forest of Arden (i.e. the Ardennes), and legend says that Bayard's mighty neigh can still be heard there. Reynard has a cousin, Maugis, who is both a warrior and a powerful magician.

Richard

Richard of Normandy, who features in the adventures of Guy of Burgundy. He may be inspired by the real-life Richard I, Duke of Normandy (933–996), who on his mother's side was a great grandson of Charlemagne.

Salomon

Also called Saloman of Brittany. He has a comrade in arms called **Estult**, and may be inspired by the real Saloman, king of Brittany, who died in 874.

Thiery

Also named Thierry, Terry, or Theoderic (of which Thiery is a shortened form), he is duke of the Ardennes and father to the paladin Berenger, as well as being the victor in the judicial duel in *The Song of Roland*.

Walter

Gualtier in French. There are two warriors of this name. Walter de l'Hum is a vassal of Roland in *The Song of Roland*, who is sent to guard his mountain flank, and is one of the last left standing. Walter d'Amulion or Turmis, along with William or Guillaume the Scot, is killed in battle attempting to rescue Oliver after he defeats Fierabras.

THE SONG OF ROLAND

The Song of Roland is among the earliest of the poems about Charlemagne to have survived and is generally considered the greatest. The story must have been well known at the time, for the author tells the tale elliptically, alluding to the backstory, and showing us personalities through their words and behaviour, assuming we will know who they are. This is a sophisticated bit of literature, not a simple story of heroics. No one comes out of the story very well. Charlemagne allows himself to be conned because he is keen to have peace, while Roland is pig-headed; Ganelon acts from hurt feelings and nearly gets away with it. The Saracens are shown as brave warriors, but they are devious. Even Oliver, the best of them all, fails to put his wisdom to good use and loses his temper.

An Embassy from Marsile

The Emperor Charlemagne felt old and tired. For seven long years he and his army had been fighting and conquering Spain, but now it had ground to a halt at the siege of Saragossa. They all longed for home. So when an embassy came from Marsile, the Saracen king of Spain, offering peace, tribute and conversion to Christianity, the temptation to accept was enormous.

Charlemagne and his court were avoiding the heat of Spain in a garden. Charlemagne sat on a golden throne in the shade of a pine tree, identifiable by his white hair and long white beard. His court stood around him, some playing backgammon or chess, the younger ones practising their sword skills. Conspicuous among the court were his paladins, the 12 peers, each of whom had a comrade who watched his back in battle and advised him in civil life. Prominent among these were Roland and Oliver. Roland, nephew and sword-bearer to the king, was impetuous, restless, obsessed with battle and brave to the point of foolhardiness. Oliver, equally brave but much more controlled, had the wisdom to think beyond the immediate moment, a useful foil to Roland's nature.

This, then, was the scene when Blancandrin, Marsile's ambassador and chief councillor, arrived. He saluted Charlemagne proudly and put his king's terms to him. If Charlemagne withdrew from Spain, Marsile would come to his court at Aachen next Michaelmas. He would be baptized in its hot springs and become a tribute-paying vassal of the emperor. As an example of the tribute, Blancandrin presented him with 700 camels, 400 mule-loads of gold and silver, cartloads of gold bezants to pay off his mercenaries, and bears, lions, hounds and hawks by the dozen. Charlemagne's first response to this apparent capitulation was to raise his hands to God in thanks. But then he bowed his head to think things through.

How did he know he could trust the pagans, he asked.

The Saracens were prepared to give him hostages, Blancandrin replied, and he was prepared to offer his own son among them.

Charlemagne called a council the next morning. He sat on his golden throne, surrounded by his best advisors, with Roland standing by his side, resting Charlemagne's naked sword, Joyeuse, on his shoulder. Charlemagne asked if he should trust the offer of the Saracens. The lords knew that once the ponderous withdrawal from Spain had taken place, it was unlikely that they would return, and they agreed that the decision needed careful thought. All except Roland, who sprang forward angrily, pointing out that the Saracens had tried this trick before. When the Franks first came to Spain, Roland had conquered large tracts of land for Charlemagne. Marsile had sent ambassadors then. The two counts sent to negotiate, Basile and Basan, had been beheaded. They must be avenged, and the war continued for as long as necessary.

Charlemagne sat in silence, stroking his long, white beard. His peers were equally silent, all except Ganelon, who stepped forward.

'Marsile says he will hold Spain as your vassal and accept the true faith. Listen to wisdom and accept his terms. Any oaf who rejects this is a reckless fool who doesn't care who dies.'

Naimes backed Ganelon, pointing out that Marsile was clearly defeated, and the war should be finished as quickly as possible. The rest of the Franks backed Naimes.

'Whom should we send?' asked Charlemagne.

Naimes, Oliver, Roland, and Archbishop Turpin volunteered, but Charlemagne rejected them all and forbade any of the other paladins to volunteer.

'Send my stepfather Ganelon,' suggested Roland, and the rest agreed that this was an excellent choice.

Ganelon reacted furiously, calling Roland mad, and vowing revenge on him if he managed to survive the embassy to Marsile. Roland replied that they needed a good man, and if the emperor agreed, he would go himself if Ganelon did not think he was up to it. Then Roland laughed in his face.

Ganelon's reaction might seem excessive, even though it hurt his pride that Charlemagne thought him more expendable than other lords. However, it was well known that he and Roland disliked each other, although the cause is not entirely clear. There were rumours that Roland was not just Charlemagne's nephew but his son, sired on his own sister, now Ganelon's wife, which, if taken seriously, made Roland's existence a daily affront to Ganelon's honour. Or it could just have been the instinctive dislike that exists between some stepfathers and their adpoted sons. The two were certainly very different types: Ganelon with his rich, elegant clothes, subtlety, and reputation for being able to talk anyone round; Roland with his single-minded faith in his strength and soldierly skills.

Ganelon turned to Charlemagne and said that he knew his duty to his lord and would go to Saragossa, even though he did not expect to return. But he asked the emperor to remember that his son Baldwin was also Charlemagne's nephew, and to make sure that he inherited what was due to him. Ganelon also vowed revenge on Roland, his companion Oliver, and, since they loved him so much, all the 12 peers. Charlemagne simply called him softhearted, and commanded him to take the wand and right glove that were the symbols of his appointment. But Ganelon fumbled taking the glove, which fell to the floor, causing gasps of superstitious horror from the court.

Ganelon set out and soon caught up with the Saracen embassy. Blancandrin rode up beside him.

'Strange man, Charlemagne,' he said. 'He's conquered a good part of the earth, and now he wants our land. Why do his counsellors push him to do this?'

'It's only Roland,' said Ganelon. 'All he cares about is fighting, and the peers support him. He's the emperor's right hand. Only his death will bring peace.'

'As for that…,' said Blancandrin, and between them they sorted out a way of getting rid of Roland.

The Betrayal

Once they reached Saragossa, Blancandrin led Ganelon to Marsile. Choosing his words with care, Ganelon presented Charlemagne's terms to the king. If Marsile would take the Christian faith, he could hold half of Spain as Charlemagne's vassal, while Roland ruled the other half. If he rejected these terms, he would be taken to Aachen in chains and executed. Enraged, Marsile snatched up a spear and threatened to kill Ganelon, who drew his sword and set his back to a tree, prepared to take as many Saracens as he could with him. But the wiser paynims, impressed by Ganelon's courage, restrained the king, while Blancandrin whispered to him that Ganelon was prepared to work with them.

Illustration by H. J. Ford for Andrew Lang's *Book of Romance* (1902).

MARSILE THREATENS GANELON WITH A JAVELIN

Marsile apologized and asked him about the emperor. 'He's over 200 years old and must be near the end of his life. Why does he keep on fighting?'

Ganelon again blamed Roland. He praised the emperor and warned that he had 20,000 knights fighting for him. Marsile replied that he could raise 400,000. Ganelon, however, advised against an overt confrontation. Instead, he recommended that Marsile should agree to all of Charlemagne's demands and wait until he left Spain. Charlemagne would leave a rearguard to hold the narrow pass at Roncevalles, while the bulk of his army crossed the Pyrenees through the Gate of Spain and returned to France. Ganelon would ensure that Roland got command of the rearguard. Then Marsile could send 100,000 of his men to ambush Roland. He must expect to lose these men, but they would reduce the number of the rearguard, and a second wave of soldiers would defeat them.

With Roland dead, both countries could finally enjoy peace. While Marsile swore on his pagan book of law to keep the deal, Ganelon took his oath on the Christian relics in the hilt of his sword, Murgleis, and was then sent back to the Franks loaded with treasure.

Charlemagne had already drawn back towards the mountains by the time Ganelon returned. As he stood outside his tent with Roland, Oliver and duke Naimes, Ganelon told him that Marsile had acceded to all his demands. He presented him with the keys to Saragossa and vast tribute. Charlemagne praised God and promised to reward Ganelon well, while the army struck camp and headed home to France, not knowing the pagan forces were close behind.

The army travelled on until it reached the high passes through the Pyrenees. There, Charlemagne called a council and asked for nominations for command of both the rearguard and the vanguard. This time Ganelon got his suggestion

SARACENS

We are used to the word 'Saracen' referring to a Muslim, particularly one who invaded and conquered Spain from the early 8th century onwards. The Middle Ages used the term in the same way, but also more widely as a general term for 'pagan'. Thus raiding Vikings could be called Saracens.

The authors and audience of the popular stories about Charlemagne and his paladins had absolutely no idea about the true nature of Islam, or of any other religion outside their own. They thought the Saracens were pagans, worshipping many idols, rather than monotheists, and authors often show them abusing or destroying these idols when things went wrong. What they did know about Saracens was that they were to be feared. These were the people who had taken most of Spain from its previous Christian rulers. They had also taken over many of the Mediterranean islands, including Sicily, and raided in Italy and France, even setting up temporary kingdoms in the south of France. Consequently, they knew Saracens could be mighty warriors and respected them as such. Yet, however noble the Saracens were, as unbelievers they were seen as doomed to hell unless they converted to Christianity. This view is summed up by the author of *The Song of Roland* in the bald statement, 'the pagans are wrong, the Christians are right'.

In the re-telling of the stories that follows, the terms 'Saracens' and 'paynims' (an old form of the word 'pagan') have been used for the non-Christian foes that give Charlemagne and his followers such a tough time.

in first, turning the tables by proposing Roland for the rearguard and Ogier the Dane for the vanguard.

Roland sneered at Ganelon. 'Do you think I would let the glove of office fall and grovel as you did? I will not let the family down, and every lost man will be paid for with the sword.'

Oliver and the paladins volunteered to go with him, which Roland accepted, but he dismissed Charlemagne's offer of half of the army to support him, saying 20,000 Franks would be ample.

Charlemagne wept with foreboding, but let his nephew go.

The Pass of Roncevalles

At Roncevalles, Roland sent Walter de l'Hum with 1,000 men up into the hills to patrol the heights, while the rest of his forces held the pass. Soon, the Franks heard the noise of the Saracens' advance. Oliver, who sat on his horse in the pass, turned to Roland and said that battle was on its way.

'May God grant it is so,' Roland replied. 'We'll do our duty by the king. There'll be no mocking stories about us. Pagans are wrong and Christians are right.'

Oliver had seen how overwhelming the size of the Saracen army was, and now he urged Roland to sound his famous horn, Oliphant, and summon Charlemagne. Roland refused, saying he would not risk his own and his country's reputation by asking for help. Instead, he would dye his sword, Durendal, in the blood of the enemy. If they were seriously outnumbered, well, that was the way he liked it. The Franks all vowed to do or die.

Archbishop Turpin called the troops together to bless them and hear their confessions. He told them that if they died in this fight they would be martyrs and go directly to Paradise. Then they signed themselves with the cross and, on Roland's orders, advanced at a walking pace. Then, giving Charlemagne's battle cry of 'Mountjoy', they charged at the advancing Saracens. Marsile's nephew Aelroth shouted out that the rearguard had been betrayed and let down, and that France would be disgraced that day. Charlemagne would lose his right-hand man. This was too much for Roland, who spurred his horse, Veillantif, forward and shattered the man's spine with his lance, throwing him dead from his horse.

'First blood to us!' Roland cried, 'We're in the right and this miscreant is wrong!'

Oliver was then attacked by Marsile's brother Falsaron and dispatched him with equal efficiency. One by one the Peers engaged with the enemy until general battle was joined. The Franks killed the flower of the Saracen army, dealing mighty blows. Roland was prominent among them, Durendal biting right and left. The Saracen knight Chernabules spurred at him and was cleft between the eyes. Down went Durendal through the chain mail, body, and organs, through the saddle and into the horse, leaving both dead on the field.

Oliver's fighting skill was not far behind, but his spear broke with the force of his blows. Undaunted, he kept up the slaughter using just the stub.

Roland saw him and called out, 'What are you up to? This isn't the time for using sticks,' and gave him a chance to draw Hauteclere, his shining sword. Many more such deeds were seen on the French side, until at last, storms and earthquakes shook the lands, and darkness came at noon as if it was Judgement Day. The Saracens were defeated, although at great cost.

The Second Assault

The surviving French searched the field to tend to their wounded and count their many dead. But as they did this, a second, even greater Saracen army under Marsile came riding up the gorge.

'Ganelon's treason is plain,' shouted Roland, as 20 squadrons of Saracens appeared.

'Strike on, good knights!' cried Archbishop Turpin as he dealt the first blow, cleaving through the magic, jewelled shield of Abisme. He then reminded his warriors that Paradise awaited them.

Outnumbered, one by one the paladins fell, to be avenged by Roland, Oliver or Turpin. Finally, only 60 Franks were left alive. At last Roland recognized the seriousness of the situation and consulted with Oliver. How, he asked, do we get news to Charlemagne? Should he sound his horn? Oliver replied that to blow it now would bring disgrace on them all; it was not the action of a brave man. Roland was puzzled by his anger, so Oliver explained. Roland would not blow Oliphant at the right time when Oliver advised it, and now he could see that prudence is better in a vassal than recklessness. If Charlemagne had been recalled the battle would have been won. Now Roland would die and France be put to shame. Before the evening fell, Charlemagne would have lost good lords and their friendship would be over. Archbishop Turpin spotted the two comrades quarrelling and rode up to them. He settled the argument by pointing out that although Charlemagne would be too late to save them, he would be able to avenge their deaths and give them a Christian burial. So Roland put Oliphant to his lips and blew a mighty blast.

Illustration by H. J. Ford for Andrew Lang's *Book of Romance* (1902).

ROLAND WINDS HIS HORN IN THE VALLEY OF RONCESVALLES

The horn call echoed over the steep mountain passes until it reached the ears of Charlemagne and his army 30 leagues away.

'Our men are fighting!' he said.

'If anyone but you said that,' said Ganelon, 'I'd call it a lie.'

'That's Roland's horn,' said Charlemagne, 'and he only ever blows it in battle.'

'There's no battle,' said Ganelon. 'You're getting old and childish. You know Roland, he'll sound that horn all day, just chasing after a hare. He's showing off to the peers. Who'd dare attack him? Let's press on to the comforts of home.'

But Duke Naimes agreed with Charlemagne. The emperor ordered the army's own horns sounded, and they turned back to ride to Roland's aid.

The Death of Roland

Back in the battle, Roland had burst a vein in his temple from blowing his horn, but still he rode into the fray, picking out Marsile for single combat. With a stroke of Durendal, he sheered off the king's right hand. At this, Marsile and many of the remaining Saracens

Roland kills the Saracen king Marsile with a single blow. Roland's death is shown at the bottom of the picture. Musée Condé, Chantilly, ms 722, f 111r. (Bridgeman Art Library)

took flight. But a few remained, led by Marsile's uncle Marganice. He drove his spear through Oliver's back so hard that the tip came out through his chest. Despite being mortally wounded, Oliver struck back, and his sword went through Marganice's jewelled helmet, splitting the skull.

Then Oliver returned to the fray, striking out wherever he could. As he did this, he called for Roland to come to his aid. Roland rode up and saw his friend pale from loss of blood. In fact, Oliver had lost so much blood that he could no longer see clearly, and in his battle fury, he struck out at Roland. Humbly and gently, Roland asked if he meant to attack him. Oliver begged forgiveness. He knew who he was now that he could hear him, and never meant to hurt him. The two friends, reconciled, embraced. Then Oliver, now blind and deaf, dismounted, knelt, and prayed for God's blessing on Charlemagne, France, and most of all, Roland. Then his heart broke and his helmeted head bowed in death.

Roland slumped in the saddle, mourning his dear friend's death. Then Walter de l'Hum came down from his mountain post, badly wounded and with all his men killed. Now only Walter, Turpin, and Roland remained alive, but they had killed so many foes that the Saracens did not dare to attack them. Instead they tried to kill them from a distance with arrows and lances. Walter fell dead, pierced by many arrows. Then Turpin and Roland had their horses killed beneath them. The two warriors stood back to back, and Roland blew his horn again. The vein he had burst in his temple was taking its toll, and the horn sounded more feebly now.

Nevertheless, the sound reached Charlemagne, who hurried on. Once again, he had all his trumpets sounded. The paynims heard the sound of the oncoming army and turned and fled, leaving Roland and Turpin on the field. But Turpin had received a head wound and collapsed on the field. Roland, without his Veillantif, could not pursue the fleeing enemy, so instead he gently tended to the dying archbishop. He then gathered up the bodies of the dead paladins, laying them in a row by Turpin, so that he could give them one last blessing before he died.

Roland knew he did not have long left, as the burst vein in his temple throbbed. His thoughts turned again to his personal reputation. He wanted to die advancing towards Spain and dominating the field, so he turned south and climbed a hillock. The exertion was almost too much, and at the top he fell, fainting. A Saracen, who had been feigning death, spotted him there and saw an opportunity to return home bearing Durendal. But even in that state, Roland revived as he felt Durendal being eased from his hand. He raised Oliphant and shattered both the jewelled horn and the coward's skull with a mighty blow.

Roland blows Oliphant (right) and tries to break Durendal (left) while a hand comes down from Heaven to receive his fealty. Charlemagne window, Chartres Cathedral, 13th century. (Sonia Halliday Photographs / Alamy)

Then, seeing the danger to his sword, he staggered to his feet and tried, repeatedly, to shatter its blade on the rocks. But the steel was too good; he could not even mark it. He was desperate that his fine sword, with its precious relics in its hilt – St Peter's tooth, St Basil's blood, St Denis' hair and part of the Virgin's robe – should not fall into pagan hands. But his death was near, and all he could do was lie down with Oliphant and Durendal hidden beneath his body. He carefully lay facing Spain, so that Charlemagne and his court would see he died a conqueror. Then he made his final prayers. As he lay dying, he offered his glove in fealty up to Heaven, and the archangel Gabriel himself descended to take it and his soul to Paradise.

Charlemagne's Dream

When Charlemagne arrived, all he found was a field littered with pagan and Christian dead, and in the distance, the cloud kicked up by the fleeing Saracen army. Leaving four lords to protect the bodies from man

and beast, Charlemagne and his army rode in hot pursuit. Evening drew in, and they were still not near them, but Charlemagne dismounted and prayed that the sun should be stayed in its course. His guardian angel, with whom he often spoke, came to tell him that his prayer was granted. The day would last as long as he needed.

The Franks finally caught the Saracens at Val Tenebros, either killing them or driving them to the banks of the nearby Ebro River. Even then there was no escape, for most who took to the water drowned in their heavy armour or were swept away. Once again Charlemagne knelt in prayer, and when he rose from his knees the sun had finally set. The emperor and his exhausted army slept where they were in their armour, leaving their horses to graze on the grass.

As Charlemagne slept, a dream came to him, a portent of the great battle that was to come, in which he and his army had to battle bears, fierce leopards, dragons, and vipers, and more than 30,000 griffins that hurled themselves at him. Fire descended from the sky, setting light to their lances.

The Final Battle

Marsile made it back to Saragossa, faint from loss of blood after Roland cut off his hand. His queen, Bramimonde, wept over his wounds, then ran to the altar of their gods, Apollyon, Termagaunt, and Mahound. She threw down the idols, and had them broken up and thrown in a ditch, rejecting them for having let the Saracens down.

As the remaining pagans rallied for one last battle, Charlemagne and his troops woke up and galloped back to Roncevalles. Charlemagne remembered that Roland had boasted that if he ever died on foreign soil, he would be found lying ahead of all the rest of the dead. On the hill where Roland died, Charlemagne spotted the marks made by Durendal as Roland tried to break it, and thus found his body. Grieving over the great losses he had sustained and the weakening it meant for his kingdom, he ordered the fallen Christians to be buried in a single grave with a great mound raised over them.

Only the bodies of Roland, Oliver, and Turpin were excepted. Their hearts were wrapped in silk and placed in a white marble coffer. Their bodies were bathed in wine and spices, wrapped in deer-hide, and readied for transport back to France to be buried. Then the army rode back down to the Spanish plain to meet the remaining Saracen army.

The Dream of Charlemagne

Illustration by H. J. Ford for Andrew Lang's *Book of Romance* (1902).

OPPOSITE
Before his final battle with the Saracens in *The Song of Roland*, Charlemagne had a symbolic dream where he and his troops are attacked by dragons, griffins and wild beasts while storms rage.

The pagans had received reinforcements led by the magnificent emir Baligant, and a mighty battle lay ahead. Unusually, both the leaders took part in the melee themselves. Each shouted their battle cry: 'Mountjoy!' from Charlemagne and 'Precieuse!', (the name of his sword) from Baligant. They recognized each other in the fray from these cries, and met in single combat. Baligant brought his sword down on Charlemagne's head, cutting through the helmet and exposing the skull beneath. Charlemagne bowed his head and almost fell, but he had God on his side, and the archangel Gabriel stood behind him. This was enough to rally him, and raising his sword, Joyeuse, he brought it down in turn on the emir's head, splitting it down to his beard.

Not surprisingly, the Saracens all fled at their leader's death. Seeing the situation was helpless, Bramimonde surrendered Saragossa to the vengeful Franks. The city was ransacked, and all of the remaining false idols smashed. Its inhabitants were offered the choice of conversion or death, all except Bramimonde, who was to be led back to France, to be converted through reason and love.

Trial by Combat

Finally, the army sadly returned to Aachen. Charlemagne called a court to witness the trial of Ganelon, but it was no open and shut case. Ganelon argued his case well and denied treason against his lord. He had served Charlemagne long and faithfully. Roland, he pointed out, hated him, and by putting him forward for the embassy to Marsile, doomed him to die. He had issued a formal defiance to Roland and his supporting peers, vowing revenge.

Charlemagne and his whole court had heard him do so. Then he had faithfully carried out Charlemagne's task. What he did was not treachery, but legitimate revenge. The court withdrew to debate this point. Many supported Ganelon's point of view, particularly as Ganelon's kinsman, the mighty Pinabel, had offered to turn the whole thing into a trial by combat, and none of them wanted to face him. Roland, after all, was dead, and nothing would bring him back, whereas Ganelon was still an asset to the empire. This was the advice they took to Charlemagne, who furiously accused them of treachery.

The village of Roncevalles, high in the Pyrenees, in Navarra, Spain, now has a Battle Square with a monument to the great battle fought by Charlemagne's paladins. (Photograph courtesy of the Reyno de Navarra Tourism Archive)

Thiery, the only one to have stood against the barons' views, then came forward and presented a differing interpretation. Roland was acting as Charlemagne's agent at the time of his death, and should thus have been protected from revenge, even if he had harmed Ganelon. Ganelon's crime was therefore treachery to Charlemagne, and the punishment for that was death. Thiery offered to defend this view with his sword, and as challenger, gave his glove to Charlemagne. Pinabel, as expected, came forward to accept the challenge, and passed his glove to Charlemagne to show this.

While the two contestants went off to pray for success, the field of combat was prepared, with Ogier the Dane as marshal. Soon, the combat began. Pinabel outweighed and had a longer reach than Thiery, and at first the fight clearly went his way. As their swords clashed and battered against each other's shields, Pinabel tried to make a deal with Thiery. If Thiery would cede the

Close up of the monument to the battle of Roncevalles. (Photograph courtesy of the Reyno de Navarra Tourism Archive)

fight so that Ganelon was acquitted, Pinabel would become Thiery's vassal and richly reward him. Thiery rejected this firmly, and the fight continued. As Charlemagne prayed that justice would be done, Pinabel slashed Thiery across the face, and his blood flowed red on the green grass. But Thiery gathered his strength, and with one counter-blow to the head, he struck Pinabel dead.

Ganelon was thus condemned to the traditional traitor's death – to have each limb tied to a stallion, and to be dragged by them until he was torn apart. Justice having been done, Charlemagne retired for the night, but not for rest. Once more the archangel Gabriel appeared and told him that King Vivien had been besieged by paynims. Charlemagne and his army must now ride to their rescue. Charlemagne wept and plucked at his long, white beard. 'Oh God,' he cried, 'how wearisome my life is!'

THE SONG OF ROLAND AND HISTORY

During Charlemagne's reign, the Saracens made constant incursions into his land, but in general he was content to let his people shelter behind the Roman walls of their cities and leave it to his counts to drive the raids back beyond the Pyrenees. This changed when a group of Saracen lords, led by the governor of Barcelona, Sulayman Yaqzan ibn 'al-'Arabi came to his court and asked him to help them against their overlord. The fact that Charlemagne would be fighting for one group of Saracens against another did not stop the pope from sending a message that he was praying for an angel sent by God to lead the Frankish army against the infidel and to allow the troops a victorious return to their homeland. In the spring of 778, Charlemagne, then only 36 rather than the white-bearded ancient of our story, set out at the head of an army. He besieged Saragossa, whose governor now reneged on his agreement to surrender to him. After some six weeks Charlemagne gave up and returned home, to deal with some Saxons who had taken the opportunity to revolt.

The chronicler Einhard tells us that on the way back, the rearguard of the army was ambushed by the Basques, who killed the Franks to a man, looted the baggage and escaped with it under cover of the falling dusk. The Basques were lightly armed and could escape over the rugged terrain where the more heavily armed Franks could not follow. 'What is more, this assault could not be avenged there and then, for, once it was over, the enemy dispersed in such a way that no one knew where or among which people they could be found.'

He also tells us that among the killed were 'Hruodlandus, prefect of the march of Brittany'. This person, mentioned in a few documents of doubtful authenticity as a close aide of the king, and about whom we know very little else, was to develop into the Roland of legend.

The Basques, who were Christian by this date, were transformed into the Saracens. However, there is some evidence from the Arabic chronicles written by Charlemagne's enemies that there may actually have been some Saracens with the Basques, and one of the aims of the ambush may have been to recapture some Saracen prisoners. Although Charlemagne himself never returned to Spain, his son did, and the area immediately to the south of the Pyrenees was added to the empire.

As for the barbaric means of Ganelon's execution, this really was the punishment for treason and was on the statute books in France and used right up to the time of the French Revolution in 1789.

Roland and Oliver

Interest in the two greatest warriors in *The Song of Roland* led to curiosity about their backstory, prequels telling us how and where they grew up, how they met and became firm friends and their deeds before their deaths at Roncevalles. As usual with these stories there are several, often conflicting, versions.

The First Meeting

Roland did not have an easy childhood. His mother, the king's sister who is given various names including Bertha and Gisela, had married Milo, a brave knight but of modest birth. The marriage was against the king's wishes and the couple had to flee the court, some say to Italy, others to France, where they lived in poverty. There are various accounts of how Roland came to Charlemagne's attention. In one, his mother was now widowed and starving, so the boy Roland marched into the king's hall and helped himself to all the best food for her. Impressed by this fearless behaviour, the king asked who the unknown boy was, and, discovering he was his nephew, took him under his wing.

Roland repaid Charlemagne's generosity by saving his life in various battles. In one he was still too young to be a knight and was forbidden to fight the Saracens who had invaded Italy. He and the other squires, including Ogier the Dane, watched as the enemy got the upper hand and the Oriflamme, the standard of France, fell. The squires could not stand by and watch this, so, arming themselves from the fallen, they dashed to the rescue, saving both the king and the day. Charlemagne rewarded them all with knighthood.

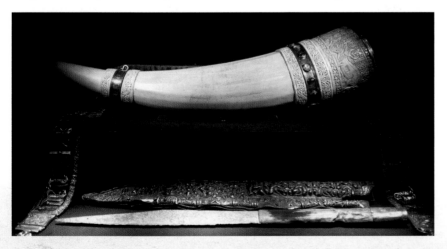

An oliphant or hunting horn. This ivory horn, although dating from *c.*1000, is known as 'The Horn of Charlemagne' and is in the Treasury of Aachen Cathedral. The hunting knife in front of it does date from the age of Charlemagne, although the sheath is from a later period. (PRISMA ARCHIVO / Alamy)

Oliver grew up in a tightly knit family, headed by Girart of Vienne, his uncle. As so often happened in these stories, Charlemagne and his queen had behaved very badly to this family, and as a result they had revolted. This led to a long siege of Vienne. Sieges seemed to have been quite relaxed affairs, and one day Roland was out hawking when his bird flew off and was captured by Oliver and his beautiful sister Aude, who had been watching events from the walls of Vienne. Swinging his hawking glove to show his peaceful intentions, Roland asked for his hawk back and lost his heart to Aude. Chivalrously, Oliver rode out of the city to return the hawk.

Later it was decided that the only way to end the siege was through a decisive single combat, and Roland and Oliver were chosen as each side's champion. Equally matched, they fought to a standstill and then were parted by a miraculous cloud, while a divine voice ordered them to make peace and go and fight the enemy in Spain. The peace was sealed by the betrothal of Roland and Aude, and the two paladins became inseparable friends.

Although Oliver is always there in the stories, fighting alongside Roland, he is not as fully realized a character. It may be significant that although the siege of Vienne seems to have been inspired by the siege of the city in 870 by Charles the Bald, grandson of Charlemagne, Oliver is one of the few paladins who is not known to be based on a real historical figure.

Fierabras the Giant

The most famous adventure of Roland and Oliver, after the battle of Roncevalles, is their conflict with the Saracen giant Fierabras, a story adapted into many languages (including at least four medieval English versions and one in Irish), which remained popular for centuries. A German version first printed in 1533 was still in print in the 19th century, eventually being turned into an opera by Schubert in 1823.

The story begins after the Saracen king Balan has sacked Rome and taken the holy relics of the Crucifixion back with him to Spain. Charlemagne invaded Spain to get the relics back, only to find that Balan had a son, Fierabras, king of Alexandria (the name, which appears in forms such as Ferumbras in some English versions, means 'proud [i.e. strong] in the arm'). He was a giant, stronger than any other man. Fierabras rode up to Franks' camp and challenged any man to fight him, or six or seven together if they preferred. Charlemagne asked Roland to accept the challenge, but Roland pointed out that when the young knights had been close to defeat the day before and Oliver badly wounded, Charlemagne had sneered at them.

Charlemagne then found that no one was prepared to take on an opponent like Fierabras. When the news reached Oliver, he insisted on dragging himself off his sickbed, and despite the

Oliver finds Fierabras resting under a tree. (British Library)

37

fact that his wounds were still bleeding, he armed himself. Roland regretted his hasty words to his uncle when he saw how they endangered his friend. Charlemagne refused to let Oliver fight, but Ganelon insisted he be allowed to. Behaving towards each other with the utmost courtesy and chivalry, Oliver and Fierabras fought, first one, then the other getting the upper hand. Each tried unsuccessfully to convert the other to their faith. Finally, Oliver slashed the giant across the stomach, nearly disembowelling Fierabras. Fierabras conceded defeat, offering to convert if he was spared.

Oliver carefully bound Fierabras's wounds and put him on a horse to lead him back to the Frankish camp. But as he did so, the Saracens treacherously broke the traditional truce that went with single combat and ambushed Oliver. Roland and his troop dashed to the rescue, but this only resulted in two more peers, Gerard and Geoffrey, being captured and taken prisoner to Aigremore, the fort of Fierabras's father Balan. Meanwhile Fierabras was taken in by the Franks and baptized. When they saw him stripped to submerge himself in the baptismal pool, they were amazed that Oliver could have overcome one so strong. What happened next belongs in the following chapter on Guy of Burgundy.

The Giant Ferragus

Some time later, Roland had his own encounter with a giant, called Ferragus (or Ferragut), sent against Charlemagne by the emir of Babylon. He challenged Charlemagne to send him knights in single combat. Ogier the Dane went first. Ferragus did not even try to fight him, but simply picked him up in one hand, tucked him under his arm and carried him off to prison. Next, Reynard met the same fate. Then Constantine and Hoel ended up tucked under each arm, as did the next two sent. While Charlemagne sat aghast, not knowing what to do next, Roland came and demanded the right to fight Ferragus.

As usual, Charlemagne did not want to risk his best knight, and as usual Roland eventually got his own way. Rather than meet him sword to sword, however, Roland armed himself with a great staff. He used this to fend off the giant, and kept him from picking him up, but he could not defeat him. By midday they had fought themselves to a standstill and agreed to make a truce and rest for a while. Roland made the giant comfortable, even bringing a large stone for him to rest his head on, and after Ferragus had slept, Roland got him talking.

Why, he asked, could he not wound him in any way? Ferragus, obviously no brighter than most giants, revealed that

Roland fights Ferragus. The 12th century column from the palace of the Kings of Navarre in Estrella, Spain, on the Pilgrims' Way to Compostela. Roland's spear can be seen piercing Ferragut's only vulnerable spot, his navel, on the left. (age fotostock / Alamy)

Giants were common foes in the stories of Charlemagne and the Paladins. Illustration by Gustave Dore.

he was invulnerable except in his navel. After a debate about their different religions, which they agreed to settle by seeing who won the fight, they started the combat again. Roland only just managed to ward off a mighty blow from Ferragus by blocking it with his staff, which was cut through. Ferragus then fell on top of Roland, and it looked like the end for him, but Roland found the strength to drive the piece of the broken staff he still held into the giant's navel, and the fight was over.

Durendal

We do not know the meaning of the name of Roland's sword, Durendal, but we are no worse off than the writers of the original stories. Guesses were being made by the 12th century. In modern times, scholars have suggested derivations from a wide variety of languages including Breton, German, Spanish, and Arabic. The most convincing suggestion is that the name is related to the word 'enduring', suggesting its unbreakability, although an Arabic term meaning 'master of stone' is also a possibility. The Arabic would also refer to the way that the dying Roland wanted to destroy the sword so it would not fall into the hands of the enemy. Even striking it against a rock could not break it, although it shattered the stone. Local legend says that the strange cleft in the cliffs in the Pyrenees that marks the border between France and Spain known as Roland's Breach was caused by his attempts to break the blade. Certainly the French audience of *The Song of Roland* would have recognized the first syllable as their word for 'hard', and 'giving hard strokes' was one of the medieval interpretations of the name.

The most widely spread story of its origin is that when still a youth Roland won the sword at the battle of Aspremont by killing the Saracen Eaumont and taking it from him. When Charlemagne made him a knight, he girded him with the sword. Eaumont is also the source of Roland's famous ivory horn, Oliphant, and of his horse, Veillantif.

Caxton, however, in his *Lyf of the Most Noble and Crysten Prynce, Charles the Grete*, tells us that there were once three brothers with the obviously foreign names Galaus, Munificans, and Agnisiax who each made three swords. Agnisiax, the youngest, made Baptism, Plourance ('weeping'), and Grabam, the three swords that Fierabras carried; Munificans made Durendal, Sauvognye, and Ogier's Cortana, while Galaus made Floberge, Reynard's sword, Oliver's Hauteclere, and Charlemagne's Joyeuse. Other provenance stories say that Charlemagne won the sword from a Saracen in his youth and later gave it to Roland; that an angel gave it to Charlemagne to give to Roland; that Durendal, Cortana and Joyeuse were all made by Morgana le Faye; that Durendal was made by Wayland the Smith of Germanic myth (some texts make Munificans a brother of Wayland); while for later writers it was the ancient sword of Hector of Troy.

What is consistent is the idea that the sword is foreign and usually old. There may be good reason for this. Archaeological analysis has shown that during the early medieval period the quality of swords in the West declined. This was because the massive Muslim expansion from the Arab peninsula and conquest of the Middle East interrupted the trade routes that had brought the best steel, made in Afghanistan and India, to the West, and they had to make do with much more brittle iron. Thus old and/or Saracen swords might well be much stronger, sharper, and less likely to break.

There are various stories about what eventually happened to the indestructible Durendal. The pragmatic Icelanders, in their version of events, have it thrown into a bog, while another northern version has Roland holding on to the sword so tightly that even in death it could not be taken from his hand. Only when his lord, Charlemagne, tried to remove it did he render up his sword, as a vassal should. Charlemagne kept the hilt for its relics, but cast the blade into a nearby stream, for no one else was worthy to wield it.

What was claimed to be Durendal was on show in the church of St Romain in Blaye, near Bordeaux, where Roland was said to have been buried, until at least 1466, although possession was also claimed by the church at Roncevalles (which also claimed to have Oliphant, as did churches at Toulouse, Aachen and Rocamadour). Another legend says that Durendal was saved from the wrong hands with the help of St Michael, who flung it away so that it flew all the way to Rocamadour in France, where it can still be seen stuck in the cliff face.

According to the legend, in order to save it from the Saracens, the archangel Michael threw Durendal all the way to the pilgrim town of Rocamadour in the Lot region of France, where it can still be seen stuck in the cliff. (Photograph courtesy of Office de Tourisme, Cour du Prieuré 46110 Carennac, France)

Guy of Burgundy

Guy of Burgundy (Guy de Bourgogne in French) is one of the less famous Paladins, but he plays a central role in the events that follow Oliver's defeat of Fierabras, so he deserves a chapter of his own. After Oliver was treacherously ambushed by the Saracens and taken captive, attempts were made to rescue him, but these had only resulted in the death of yet more knights and the capture of Gerard and Geoffrey, despite a five-mile chase that only ended with darkness. The Saracens carried off their prisoners to their fortress at Aigremore, the headquarters of Balan, the father of Fierabras. When Balan heard of Fierabras's defeat, he raged and demanded to know who had defeated him. The Saracens pointed out Oliver. Realizing that if the prisoners were known to be three of the paladins they would be immediately killed, Oliver gave a false name and said that he and his companions were poor knights of little worth. Balan wanted to kill them anyway and ordered them tied to a pillar for target practice. He was reminded that they could be used in exchange for his son, so instead they were thrown into a deep dungeon. This was a cave that slowly filled with salt water as the tide rose. The salt was agony in Oliver's wounds, but Gerard and Geoffrey managed to haul him up onto a ledge of rock so he escaped drowning.

Balan's daughter Floripas heard the uproar of these events and came with her 12 attendant maidens to ask her father what was happening, dazzling all who saw her with her beauty. Balan told her about the capture of her brother. She was curious about the prisoners and went to see them, but the jailer barred her way, saying that the foul dungeon was no place for her. Besides, Balan had forbidden anyone to go near it. However, like many of the Saracen princesses in the romances, Floripes was tough and resourceful. She picked up a staff and laid the jailer out with a single blow. Also like other Saracen princesses, she had a weakness for Frankish knights and after talking to the prisoners for some time, offered to help them escape in return for a favour to be claimed later. They gave their word, and Floripas lowered a rope down into the dungeon, pulling them up one after another, and took them through a secret passageway to her chambers.

Floripas outside the tower where the knights are kept prisoner. (British Library)

Her chamberlain recognized the knights, and threatened to tell her father. Floripas beckoned her over to the large window overlooking the sea, as if to consult her, and calmly pushed her out of the window, to the delight of the knights. When she had seen them washed, fed, and treated for their wounds, Floripas reminded them of their bargain. During the Saracen attack on Rome, she explained, she had seen Guy of Burgundy fight in single combat and lost her heart to him. What she wanted in return for their rescue was for them to arrange her marriage with him. They promised to do all they could.

Back in the Frankish camp, Renier, Oliver's father, wanted to go to Balan to negotiate his son's release. Charlemagne, rather arbitrarily, said Roland should go instead, and should demand the return of both the prisoners and also the sacred relics looted from Rome. Roland objected that this would be running his head into a noose. One after another Naimes, Basin, Thiery, Ogier, Richard of Normandy, and Guy of Burgundy all backed up Roland's view, and each was summarily ordered to join in the negotiation group. The next morning they reluctantly set out.

Meanwhile, Balan had also sent a group to negotiate Fierabras's release. Inevitably, the two groups met and fought, with the paladins victorious. When they appeared before Balan, the paladins arrogantly made their demands

The Tower of Floripas, now in the middle of a reservoir, but once on the banks of the River Tagus, Estremadura, Spain, supposedly where the events of the story took place. (Photo by Marbregal)

known. Not surprisingly, Balan was enraged and determined to put them to death. Floripas then staged a strategic entry. When her father asked her what she thought should be done with the knights, she coolly answered, 'Cut off their heads, and burn them'; but, she pointed out, it was dinner time, so he should pass them on to her to look after and deal with them later, rather than have to watch an execution on an empty stomach.

As the Franks followed her to her chambers, the elderly Naimes commented on her extraordinary beauty and said it would be a lucky man who got her. The insensitive Roland responded, 'What hundred thousand devils made you say that at a time like this?'

Once the paladins were reunited in Floripas' chambers, she presented them all with her deal. The others heartily endorsed the deal, but Guy's initial reaction was, 'God forbid that I take any wife but the one that Emperor Charles gives me,' although he was eventually persuaded to agree.

On Floripas' advice, the paladins armed themselves, and that night they drove the Saracens out of the keep with their sudden, unexpected attack. While they now held the keep, they had no food reserves, and knowing this Balan besieged them. This problem was solved by a daring sortie attacking Balan's supply train, but although it solved their food shortages, Guy himself was taken prisoner in the raid. Floripas was understandably distressed, but rather than swoon away, she issued an ultimatum. Either they rescue Guy within two days, or she would surrender the castle to her father.

Meanwhile, recognizing Guy as the root cause of all his trouble, Balan decided to hang him in front of the castle, hoping that when the Franks made a rescue sortie he could capture the lot of them. The scheme worked, in so far as the paladins made their sortie as Guy was led bound and blindfolded to the gallows. But Balan had not reckoned on the prowess of the peers. Roland saved Guy from the gallows, despite the springing of the ambush, and they cut their way back into the tower. Guy, who had armed himself with the weapons of a fallen Saracen, performed prodigious feats of valour while Floripas cheered him on from a window.

The Saracens next decided to take the castle by force and, bringing up their siege engines, they captured the outer walls of the castle and began to assault the keep. There seemed to be nothing that the paladins could do to prevent the keep from being battered down too, until the ever-resourceful Floripas came up with a solution. She said that she had the keys to her father's treasury, which was full of gold. The paladins soon found that gold bars make excellent projectile weapons. They not only had heft, but chaos erupted wherever they landed, as the Saracen soldiers fought each other for them.

During the disturbance this caused, Richard of Normandy managed to slip out of the keep. Despite hair-raising adventures avoiding the Saracens, he reached Charlemagne, who brought his troops to the rescue. The siege was soon broken, and Balan captured. Although Fierabras begged for his

father's life, Balan was executed after he refused to be baptized and assaulted the priest. Floripas, however, was baptized. When she stripped off for the total immersion rite, as it was then practised, everyone there was stunned by her beauty. Even Charlemagne, old as he was, was affected by it. After that she and Guy were married. She handed over the sacred relics that her father had stolen. In return Charlemagne made her and Guy king and queen of Spain, with Guy immediately handing over part of the country to Fierabras as his under-king.

That is the end of the story, but it lives on. Every year, several towns in Spain and Portugal have pageants showing the conversion of Floripas. The Jesuits, founded by a Spaniard, also made use of the story and took it with them on their missions, seeing it as an excellent example of a story that showed their religion overcoming all adversity to convert the heathen. As a result, folk plays based on this and other Charlemagne stories are still performed in places as widely separated as Mexico and Cochin in India.

OGIER THE DANE

Unusually complex and contradictory stories are associated with Ogier the Dane, who in the past was one of the most popular of Charlemagne's paladins. In the early stories he is very much the epic action hero, but later on he became a major figure of fantasy. He is also one of the longest-lasting paladins, appearing in the earliest texts and still having stories written about him in the 19th century.

A 16th century mural of Holger Danske/Ogier the Dane in the church at Skævonge, Denmark. (PD)

We first meet him, under his original name, in Notker the Stammerer's *Life of Charlemagne*. This is a distorted version of real history, written some 100 years after the actual events. Charlemagne's brother Carloman had originally inherited the southern part of Frankia from their father Pepin the Short. In 771 Carloman died aged only 20, some said a suspiciously early age. Whatever the cause of his death, Charlemagne took over as ruler of his lands. Even before this, Carloman's widow Giberga had fled with her two small children to the lands of Desiderius, prince of Lombardy, after which they disappear from history. Accompanying her was a Frankish nobleman called Autcarius, according to the Latin chronicle the *Liber Pontificalis*. This man was actually in charge of Verona at the time of the siege of Pavia, but there is no doubt that he is the original of the 'Otkerus' (i.e. Otker) who appears at Pavia in Notker's text, and that this is the same person later known as Ogier the Dane.

According to Notker's version, Otker was one of Charlemagne's chief nobles, who had quarrelled with him (a story element that appears in later stories of Ogier), and had fled to Lombardy and Prince Desiderius. Shut up in the impregnable fortress of Pavia, they watched the arrival of Charlemagne's besieging army from the highest tower of the city. First the baggage train arrived. Desiderius asked if Charles was in that vast army.

'Not yet,' replied Otker.

Then the foot soldiers arrived. Charles must surely be there in this great army, said Desiderius.

'Not yet, not yet,' was the reply.

Then the royal bodyguard appeared. Increasingly agitated by the sight, Desiderius asserted that Charles must be with *these* troops.

'Not yet, not yet.'

Then the bishops and other clergy who travelled with the army arrived. 'Charles *must* be here now,' said Desiderius, and the sight so terrified him that all he wanted to do was hide.

'Not yet, not yet. When you see the fields bearing iron like standing corn, then you will know that Charlemagne is here.'

Then they saw the man of iron approaching. He wore an iron helmet on his head, an iron breastplate, and iron sleeves on his arms. In his iron-gloved hands, he gripped an iron spear in the left and his unconquered sword in the right. While others do not wear iron on their thighs, so that they can more easily mount a horse, his were iron-clad, and like the rest of his army his greaves were of iron. His shield was of iron and even his horse gleamed the color of iron. In the stormy light that had descended with Charlemagne's arrival, the whole field gleamed the color of iron, and Desiderius and Otker were overwhelmed.

'That,' said Otker, 'is Charlemagne.'

Because his title 'the Dane' is unexplained in the early stories, such as *The Song of Roland*, it had been suggested that originally his French title was not 'Ogier le Danois' but 'Ogier l'Ardennois', 'Ogier from the Ardennes'. But there is not much evidence to support this idea, and right from the start he is called 'Ogier from Denmark' as often as 'the Dane'. Later on, stories were invented to explain his origin. These say that he was the son of duke Geoffrey of Denmark (a Gudfred or Godfred ruled Denmark from about 804–10 and fought Charlemagne). His father had failed in his duties as a vassal, and Charlemagne had demanded he send his son as a hostage. Ogier was imprisoned in Saint-Omer in France, but it must have been quite an easy captivity, for he was able to fall in love with the castellan's daughter and have a son, Baudoinet, by her.

When Charlemagne was called to Italy to defend Rome against the Saracens, he took Ogier along as well, to keep an eye on him. As a noble youth, noble deeds of arms came naturally to him, and when, in an episode similar to Roland's conduct at Aspremont, he saw the Oriflamme and even Charlemagne's life under threat, Ogier dashed to the rescue armed only with a club and saved the day. This heroism won him his freedom and knighthood. Some say it was at this point he won his sword Cortana (called 'the short' because its tip was missing) and his magnificent horse Broiefort, after single combat with the noble Saracen Karahue. Others say the sword was a gift from Charlemagne, or Morgana le Fay, who made it, Durendal, and Joyeuse from the same steel.

Ogier the Outlaw

In this way, Ogier became one of Charlemagne's paladins. But some years later he found himself an outlaw. His son, Baudoinet, was playing chess with Charlemagne's spoilt brat of a son, Charlot, who was a bad loser. In a fit of pique, Charlot hit Baudoinet on the head with the large chessboard and killed him. Ogier tried unsuccessfully to kill Charlot in revenge and was banished by Charlemagne. Here we see the echoes of history, for the story tells us that Ogier fled to Didier (the French form of Desiderius) in Pavia. After the taking of Pavia, Ogier took refuge in a nearby fort, where Charlemagne again besieged him. With all his men dead, Ogier had to defend it single-handed, an obviously impossible task. So he carved figures of wood, set them up on the battlements so that they appeared to be manned, and then slipped out of the fort at night. After creeping into the enemy camp under cover of darkness to make yet another unsuccessful attempt to kill Charlot, he fled again on the faithful Broiefort.

All of Charlemagne's great empire was alerted to make him a prisoner if he was found, but he evaded capture until one day bishop Turpin found the exhausted fugitive asleep in a wood. Reluctantly, Turpin arrested him and imprisoned him. Incensed by the attacks on his son, Charlemagne ordered

Statue of Holger Danske by Hans Peder Pedersen-Dan (1907) in the cellar of Kronborg Castle, Denmark, where he is said to be sleeping until his country needs him to come to its rescue. The statue faces Sweden. (Niels Poulsen mus / Alamy)

that the prisoner should be given no more than a quarter of a loaf of bread and one cup of watered wine a day. Turpin kept to the letter of Charlemagne's decree, but had an enormous loaf baked every day and a gigantic cup made, so Ogier did not starve.

Some time later, the heathen giant Brahier invaded the empire at the head of a great army of Saxons and Africans. The Franks knew that Ogier was their only hope, and broke Charlemagne's ban on mentioning his name in order to insist on his release. Ogier agreed to save the realm, but the price was Charlot's life. Charlemagne had no choice but to save his realm at the cost of his son, but as Ogier was about to decapitate Charlot, an angel came between them,

(OVERLEAF)
Ogier and Desiderius watch in horror as Charlemagne, the Man of Iron, arrives to attack Pavia.

and told Ogier that he had to be content with no more than boxing his ears.

Later, having defeated the giant, Ogier rescued a beautiful girl who turned out to be the heiress to the throne of England. Ogier married her and became king of England, before retiring, along with his old comrade in arms Benoit, to a monastery in his old age. He was eventually buried at Meaux in northern France.

The Later Tales of Ogier

From the later Middle Ages onwards, a much more romantic set of stories were told of Ogier. In these versions, Ogier is blessed by six fairies in his cradle who gave him the gifts of never fearing death; of being a great warrior who would never be beaten in a fight; that he should be famous for his courtesy; that women would love him; and finally, the gift of Morgan le Fay, that at the end of his life he should come to live with her forever in Avalon. In old age, after reigning as king in Denmark and in England, Ogier went to fight in the Holy Land. After many adventures there, and when he was 100 years old, he decided to return to France. On the way home, his ship was wrecked, and all of the crew drowned. Ogier alone struggled ashore, finding himself on a magic island. This turned out to be Avalon, where he lived happily with Morgan and Arthur. Morgan placed a ring on his finger that restored his youth. In Avalon, as in other enchanted lands, time does not pass as it does in our world, and although it seemed only a short time to Ogier, 200 years had passed in our world before he returned to France.

Home again, he found that once more pagans were threatening the land. With Ogier at the head of the army, they were soon defeated. The old king having died, Ogier was about to marry the queen and ascend the throne once held by Charlemagne. But Morgan was jealous and, at the last moment, she snatched him back to live forever with her.

The final manifestation of Ogier is as a Danish national hero. The Danish did not really start writing about Ogier until the 15th century, but then he was changed from a hero of epic or romance into a great national hero under the name of Holger Danske. This tradition reached its apogee in the highly nationalistic story published in 1845 by Hans Christian Andersen, who wrote:

The old castle of Kronenburg, where Holger Danske sits in the deep, dark cellar, into which no one goes. He is clad in iron and steel, and rests his head on his strong arm; his long beard hangs down upon the marble table, into which it has become firmly rooted; he sleeps and dreams, but in his dreams he sees everything that happens in Denmark. On each Christmas-eve an angel comes to him and tells him that all he has dreamed is true, and that he may go to sleep again in peace, as Denmark is not yet in any real danger; but should danger ever come, then Holger Danske will rouse himself, and the table will burst asunder as he draws out his beard. Then he will come forth in his strength, and strike a blow that shall sound in all the countries of the world.

TURPIN

While the image of the knight fighting for his king has become a familiar one, that of an archbishop as at home in the saddle with a sword in his hand as at the altar feels somewhat unusual these days. However, in the past people found nothing strange in a bishop who could hold mass, give the troops absolution, and then go out and slaughter paynims with the best. Indeed, as we shall see, this could happen in real life.

The archbishop Turpin and Egmeaux, Charlemagne's chaplain, writing about the emperor's life from a 1493 manuscript now held in the National Library of the Turin University. (Mary Evans)

The Charlemagne legends give us very little information about Turpin's background other than that he was archbishop of Reims, and he is described in *The Song of Roland* as a strong and mighty warrior. His real-life model seems to have been Turpin or Tulpin who was archbishop of Reims in the second half of the 8th century, and thus at the time of the battle of Roncevalles in 778. There seems to be no particular reason why he was chosen as the model for the fictional warlike bishop, although it is possible that his name became linked with some of the deeds of his immediate predecessor, Milo, who had been sent on a mission to the Basques. Milo was a controversial figure, to say the least, whose life was so irregular that he was finally deposed. He had been a soldier before becoming a bishop and was killed while hunting a wild boar.

Despite the detailed description of Turpin's noble death in *The Song of Roland*, he had an interesting afterlife. Probably the most influential text in the development of the Charlemagne legend was the *History of King Charles the Great and Roland*, supposedly written by Turpin while he was recovering from his wounds gained at Roncevalles. This chronicle, widely known as the *Pseudo–Turpin*, was probably written in the mid–12th century. It seems to have been designed to boost pilgrimages to the shrine of St James at Compostela in Galicia, northern Spain. The site became the most prestigious in medieval Western Europe, attracting pilgrims and their money from all over the Catholic world. The Way of St James (still a popular challenge for both the devout and long-distance walkers) takes pilgrims over the Pyrenees by the same route that Charlemagne would have taken, via the pass of Roncevalles, and it is no coincidence that relics of the paladins, a good source of tourist money even then, are found in places along the route the pilgrims would have followed.

The Pseudo-Turpin

In the *Pseudo-Turpin*, which has a strong religious bent to it, the main reason for Charlemagne's presence in Spain is to restore the sacred site at Compostela, where the body of St James, who was said to have first brought Christianity to Spain, had been buried. However, the Galicians had wandered from the true faith, and the body was now lost. While still in France, Charlemagne had been having dreams telling him to restore the shrine, which had been sacked by the Saracens (which did happen in real life in 997), and to follow the path of St James, the Milky Way, to where he would find the lost body of the Apostle. Thereafter, people from all over the world would flock to the restored shrine.

Responding to the divine prompting of these dreams, Charlemagne invaded Spain, besieged Pamplona, and took it after the walls crumbled in response to his prayers. The Saracens were given the choice of converting or death. After visiting the shrine of Compostela, Charlemagne destroyed all of the pagan idols and over the next three years conquered widely, using the booty to enhance the shrine of St James. He then returned to France until he heard that a North African king called Aigolant had invaded Spain and was re-conquering it for *his* faith.

Aigolant and Charlemagne met in a series of escalating battles by the River Cea. One night, before the final pitched battle, the Christian army was camped at Sahagún, by the church of the martyrs Facundus and Primitivus, which Charlemagne had had built. The knights had all prepared their weapons in advance, and had stuck their spears in the ground ready for use before they had gone to sleep. In the morning some of these spears, including that of Roland's father Milo, had miraculously taken root and sprouted bark and leaves. This turned out to be a sign of which soldiers should die in the coming battle. Although the soldiers cut the sprouted spears off near the ground, the roots remained and regrew to form a miraculous grove. (Sahagún is at a convenient stopping place on the Way of St James, and provided another tourist attraction.)

Although he was defeated, Aigolant managed to raise another army and invaded France, taking the Gascon city of Agen. He sent a message to Charlemagne, offering him great gifts if he would submit to him. Sensing both a trap and an opportunity, Charlemagne disguised himself as his own messenger, bearing an answer that Charlemagne would treat with Aigolant if he would meet him outside the city, each with only 40 men. Aigolant agreed

A 13th century window in the Chartres Cathedral depicting Charlemagne. (Sonia Halliday Photographs / Alamy)

to this, and, after spying out the weak points of the city, Charles left. Naturally the perfidious paynims did not keep to the limited number of fighters for the meeting, but nevertheless Charlemagne and his knights were able to drive him back into the city, which they then besieged.

One night, just as Charlemagne's siege engines were about to breach the walls, Aigolant and his princes managed to escape the city via the latrines that overhung the river that flows past Agen. *Pseudo-Turpin* then lists the warriors who set out into Spain after Aigolant, claiming that he himself 'with fitting exhortations inspired the faithful to fight for Christ and frequently took part in the fighting myself'.

On the night before the next battle, Charlemagne prayed to God for a sign to show which of his men would die in battle. When day broke, some had the mark of a blood-red cross on their shoulders. These men Charles left behind in a chapel. But when the battle was over and three thousand pagans but no Christians had been killed, Charlemagne returned to find that the men in the chapel were dead, proving that you cannot thwart God's will. Charlemagne proceeded to re-conquer the whole of Spain, disbanded his army and once again visited St James' shrine. There Turpin and nine other bishops dedicated the altar, and Charlemagne gave great wealth and lands to the church.

Pseudo-Turpin then tells the story of *The Song of Roland* with a few variations. One is that the reason the rearguard was defeated was that on several preceding nights some of them had got drunk and lain with women,

A Tale of Two Bishops

The life story of Odo of Bayeux, half-brother of William the Conqueror, could have been modelled on that of Turpin. Both combined their religious duties with a very active life as fighters. Both were crusaders, as Odo joined the First Crusade, although he died on his way to the Holy Land. Odo's role as a warrior is not in doubt. His seal shows him as a knight in armour, sword by his side.

There is a persistent story that priests fought with maces, as they were forbidden to shed blood. This was not true, but could perhaps have been inspired by the name of Turpin's sword – Almace – and the fact that Odo is shown in the Bayeux Tapestry in the middle of the battle of Hastings carrying what could be a mace, but is more likely to have been a staff of office. The abbey of St Denis, just outside Paris and the burial place of French kings, claimed to have Turpin's sword until at least the 18th century.

Odo played a prominent part in the successful Norman invasion of England by William the Conqueror in 1066. At the battle of Hastings, which won William the kingdom, a jongleur or minstrel called Taillefer is said to have performed feats of sword juggling and to have sung of 'Charlemagne and Roland and of Oliver and their vassals who died at Roncevalles'. He is then said to have killed an English soldier who attacked him before charging the English ranks and dying.

We know Odo was a patron of the arts. There is little doubt that he commissioned the Bayeux Tapestry, that brilliant embroidered strip-cartoon which is one of our major sources for the story of the Norman invasion and Hastings. Given the similarities between the Turpin of *The Song of Roland* and Odo's own image, it is not surprising that it has been suggested that Odo may have commissioned the writing of this great work of literary art as well.

both Christian and Saracen. Their deaths were their punishment, while the deaths of the innocent were justified by stating that it saved them from the risk of sinning in the future! Once the main battle was over, Roland blew his horn not to alert Charlemagne but to rally any survivors. It was these rallying calls that Charlemagne heard, the sound having been carried by an angel to his ears. Having captured a Saracen who had been separated from the main army, the hundred or so survivors forced him to point out the Saracen king among the surviving paynims. These remaining warriors then charged, ensuring that at least the enemy king died, even at the cost of their own lives.

Later, both Baldwin and Theoderic (i.e. the Thiery of *The Song of Roland*) in turn find the dying Roland and carry the news to Charlemagne, for Turpin, of course, is not there. He was with Charlemagne, in the middle of saying mass, when he saw a vision of the paynims' souls being taken to hell, while the Christian ones were carried up to Heaven. Charlemagne returned to Roncevalles, finding first Roland's body and then Oliver's. Oliver had been tortured to death by the Saracens, flayed, and then pegged out in the form of a cross. The body of Roland is taken to Blaye and buried in the church of St Romain, where Durendal and Oliphant are on his tomb, although Oliphant was later taken to the church of St Severin in Bordeaux, where many of the other paladins are buried. Oliver and some others were buried in Belin, not far from Bordeaux (and all, naturally, on the pilgrims' route to St James).

THE ITALIAN VERSIONS

With the dawn of the Italian Renaissance, a major change came in the type and tone of the stories told about the paladins. They stopped being epic tales about fights and touchy barons with conflicts of honour and instead became often over-the-top, literary works, written in complex verse, designed to amuse and entertain their sophisticated courtly audience through their wit and invention. Magic swords, magicians intervening after scrying from afar and many other standard elements in modern fantasy literature were introduced. This included, in Bradamante, that stalwart of the genre, the female paladin.

The complex and conflicting loves of the characters are the most important elements in these stories. The setting of Charlemagne's wars against the Saracens is used to complicate the plots, but is something that can be ignored when inconvenient. With the change in language came a change in name forms: Roland became Orlando, Reynard became Rinaldo, Maugis became Malagigi, and Durendal became Durindana. Such was the respect for the writers of the Italian Renaissance that in the 19th and early 20th centuries these were the stories most commonly translated into English and are still the most readily available. These fantastic stories have been a fruitful source for writers of melodrama and opera.

The first of these authors was Luigi Pulci, who in 1483 published *Morgante*, a rollicking tale of how Orlando overcame Saracen giants who were terrorizing a monastery, killing two and converting the third, who then became his devoted follower. The giant, the Morgante of the title, is no longer a noble infidel like Fierabras, but is the thick, comic giant of fairytale. The poem swings wildly between comedy, satire, and ribaldry before the tragedy of the final battle at Roncevalles. It leans heavily on word-play, so that even that master word-smith, Byron, only had mixed success in his translation of the first part.

Orlando Innamorato

Much better known are the linked works of Pulci's successors, Matteo Boiardo, whose unfinished *Orlando Innamorato* ('Orlando in Love') was first published in 1482, and Ludovico Ariosto's continuation, *Orlando Furioso* ('Orlando Run Mad'), which was first published in 1516. Given that the 1532 extended edition of Ariosto runs to almost 39,000 lines, it will be clear that a summary of the major plot lines of the very convoluted stories is all

Astolpho flying over fantastical lands by Gustave Dore.

that can be given here. Boiardo pulled in fantasy material from all over the place including the Arthurian stories, involving people such as Merlin in his characters' adventures.

The works open with a tournament, at which the incomparably beautiful Saracen princess, Angelica, and her brother Uberto, challenge Charlemagne's knights. Anyone Uberto vanquishes shall remain his prisoner, but if he is beaten, the victor gets Angelica. What the court does not know is that Uberto has a magic horse and an enchanted, unbeatable spear, and Angelica has a magic ring, which allows the wearer to see through magic illusion and to become invisible themselves. The first two to try their luck were Astolpho and the uncouth Ferragu. Since Astolpho was not a good jouster it was no surprise when he was unhorsed. Ferragu met the same fate, but nevertheless made sexual advances towards Angelica. This so frightened her that she slipped on her magic ring and fled, calling to her brother to meet her in the forest.

Rinaldo and Orlando, both of whom had been very struck by Angelica's charms, immediately set out after her too, and so ended up in the ridiculous situation of searching for someone invisible. In the forest were two springs, one that inspired love, the other hate. In a plot that Shakespeare seems to have recalled for *A Midsummer Night's Dream*, Angelica quenched her thirst at the spring of love. Wandering on, she found Rinaldo sleeping by the spring of hate, from which he had drunk. She immediately fell in love with him, but he

Ruggiero rescues Angelica from the Orc by Gustave Dore.

now hated her and ran off, pursued by her pleas. Orlando, still besotted with her, followed after her.

After some time Rinaldo met a weeping damsel called Flordelis, and like a good knight, he agreed to help her rescue her lover Florismart from the toils of an enchantress. As they rode through the wood, they heard a strange noise. Following it, they found a giant standing in a cave, guarding a wonderful horse: an enchanted animal, unmatched in speed, so superior to all others that it fed only on air. It was called Rabican. Beside the cave a fierce griffin was chained. As he fled Rinaldo's blows, the giant managed to release the griffin, which immediately flew up into the air, and with an eagle's scream plunged down onto Rinaldo. Over and over it swooped on him, and Rinaldo could find no way to get at it. Finally, he let it knock him off his feet. When it came down once more to grip him and plunge its beak into him, it discovered that it had been tricked by Rinaldo's apparent defeat.

By the time it realized its mistake, Rinaldo had slashed a wing off, and finally after a long struggle, he managed to kill it. Mounting Rabican, Rinaldo rode off with Flordelis to fulfill his promise to her and seek further adventures.

By this time Angelica had returned to her home. She was the daughter of the king of Cathay, and she and her father were besieged in the city of Albracca by Abrican, king of Tartary, in revenge for having been rejected by Angelica. Orlando had been defending her, but, by a series of chances, Rinaldo had ended up fighting for Abrican against the woman he was enchanted to hate. Knowing that Orlando and Rinaldo would inevitably meet in combat, and fearing for Rinaldo whom she was enchanted to love, Angelica sent Orlando off to seek and destroy the garden of the enchantress Falerina, who held many knights prisoner. Rinaldo also set out on this quest, for it was the very place that Florismart was prisoner.

The immensely strong man who was guardian of the bridge to the magical garden was too much for Rinaldo, who was taken prisoner, but Orlando managed to defy the enchantments and overcame all the dangers there, even a dragon and a siren, to set the captives free. Among them was an envoy from Charlemagne ordering his knights home again, for France had been invaded once again by Saracens. Rinaldo duly returned, but Orlando was still too fascinated by Angelica to obey even such urgent summons.

Rogero and Bradamante

The invader was Agramant, king of Africa. It had been prophesied that he would never succeed without the help of a young knight called Rogero. However, Rogero was a ward of a powerful magician, Atlantes, who, knowing the danger he was in, had Rogero in protective custody. The only way to get hold of him was to use Angelica's ring to defeat Atlantes' spells. Brunello, a dwarf who was the best thief in all Africa, undertook to steal it. Despite the fact that Angelica was besieged, he managed to do this, and the ring was used

to get Rogero out of his luxurious prison. Agramant was delighted and gave Rogero a magnificent sword, and a splendid horse called Frontino. Rogero then went to France with Agramant, and battle was joined between the two sides. In the course of the battle the troops were scattered. Rogero met in single combat with a knight who turned out to be Bradamante, Rinaldo's sister, and lost his heart to her. Rinaldo, chasing another knight, ended up back by the Fountain of Love, and drinking from it found his hate for Angelica turned to passion. Meanwhile, Angelica herself had persuaded Orlando that all hope of keeping her city from her attackers was lost, and they had embarked for France, Orlando not realizing that her motive was to get back to Rinaldo. Unfortunately, as they made their way towards France, Angelica happened to drink from the Fountain of Distain, reversing her former feelings for Rinaldo, so that she now fled from his ardent advances. The fortunes of war being what they are, they were again separated.

While Bradamante was searching through the magical forest for Rogero, she learned that he had been captured by yet another enchanter, who carried people off with the help of a winged horse. Her quest to rescue her love was helped by Melissa, an enchantress who told her that the only way to defeat the enchanter was to get hold of Angelica's ring, which would allow her to see through his enchantments. Even now, she said, Brunello was on his way with the ring on the same quest to release Rogero, so that the prophecy could be fulfilled. The two women agreed that Bradamante would let Brunello guide her into the castle, where she would kill him and take the ring. But when they arrived at the castle, which was on an unclimbable pillar of rock, Bradamante found she could not kill an unarmed man. Instead she overcame him, took the ring, and tied him to a tree. She then issued a challenge to the enchanter, who flew down on his steed, which turned out to be not a horse, but a hippogriff, with the head of an eagle, bird of prey claws, feathery wings, and the body of a horse.

With the help of the ring, Bradamante was able to defeat the enchanter, only to discover that he was Atlantes, who had set the whole thing up in order to get Rogero back into his power to protect him from the perils of war. Bradamante insisted that all the prisoners be released, but Atlantes had one more trick up his sleeve. When Bradamante tried to catch the reins of the hippogriff, it moved off again and again. Eventually all the prisoners were chasing after the beast. Finally, it allowed Rogero to grab its reins, but when he mounted it to ride it back to Bradamante, it took off and flew away with him. Thanks to the machinations of Atlantes, he ended up in the power of the evil enchantress Alcina, sister of Morgana, so lost to luxury that he forgot everything else. But Bradamante had not forgotten him, and Melissa came to her aid as she searched.

Borrowing Angelica's ring from Bradamante, she released both Rogero and Astolpho, who had also been ensnared by Alcina. Rogero and Bradamante were to undergo further separations and tribulations, but eventually Rogero was able to convert to Christianity and marry Bradamante.

HIPPOGRIFFS

The hippogriff is an invention of Ariosto's, and typical of the learned jokes his courtly audience enjoyed. In classical myth, the griffin and the horse were traditional enemies. In one of his poems, the Roman poet Virgil described the chances of a successful relationship between two particular people as unlikely as the mating of a horse and a griffin. The near worship of the classical past by educated Renaissance Italians would have made this poem familiar to Ariosto's audience, so he could amuse them by showing such an unlikely mating having taken place.

Orlando Furioso

While that was going on, Angelica had fled France to escape her importunate lovers. She ended up stranded on an island that was being harassed by a sea monster called the Orc. The inhabitants decided to sacrifice her to the monster in the hope of appeasing it. Luckily for Angelica, Rogero was flying his hippogriff back to look for Bradamante when he spotted what was happening, and in the nick of time flew down and defeated the Orc. Taking her up on the back of his hippogriff, he flew her to France, where the ungrateful woman took the opportunity to get her ring back, popped it in her mouth and disappeared. While he was trying to find her, the hippogriff got loose from the branch it was tied to and flew away, although luckily it was soon recaptured by Astolpho.

St John and Astolpho travel to the moon in Elija's Chariot by Gustave Dore.

(PREVIOUS PAGE)
Rinaldo fights the griffin guarding the horse Rabican while Flordelis looks on.

Meanwhile, Orlando was deeply affected by his frustrated love for Angelica, expressing his sorrow by wearing black armour. His melancholy turned to madness when he discovered that Angelica had fallen in love with and married a soldier she had nursed back to health after he was wounded fighting the French. He wandered the woods shrieking, and attacking anything he saw. While this was happening, Astolpho had been having adventures flying the hippogriff to many wonderful places. Eventually he reached the Earthly Paradise, and from there St John took him in Elijah's chariot up to the moon. Among many strange sights, he found a valley, full of things intangible on earth. This is the place that lovers' sighs go to, as well as many other wasted qualities, including lost opportunities. One of these lost things is good sense, something that easily evaporates, so has to be kept in sealed flasks. Astolpho found one of these that was labelled 'The Sense of the Paladin Orlando'. Orlando's flask was large and full of his lost wits.

Descending from the moon, Astolpho set out for France and the war against the Saracens. There he met Orlando, and opening the flask under his nose, let him breathe his sense back into his body. Orlando returned to sanity, and since love is a form of madness, in the process lost his infatuation for Angelica. With Orlando returned to sanity, the French, led by him and Rinaldo, were eventually able to drive the Saracens out of France.

CHILDE ROLAND

While Italian writers turned the medieval stories into fluffy sophistication, something very strange happened in Britain. In the Middle Ages, Charlemagne stories had been popular in English, both in prose and verse, but these were mostly translations or adaptations from French originals. The first evidence we have of something new in English comes from Shakespeare. In *King Lear* the nobleman Edgar is posing as Poor Mad Tom to escape persecution. As a part of his act he uses gibberish and quotes from popular song and verse. In Act IV scene 3 he says:

> Childe Rowland to the Dark Tower came,
> His word was still 'Fie, foh, and fum,
> I smell the blood of a British man'.

The questions we are left with are: who is this Childe Rowland, what is the Dark Tower, and do the following lines have anything to do with Childe

Burd Ellen runs widdershins round the church.

67

Robert Browning, author of the poem *Childe Roland to the Dark Tower Came*.

Rowland, or are they the results of Tom's madness, pulled in from a giant killer story?

'Childe' is an old term for a young knight, and Roland or Rowland (once the standard English spelling) is so firmly identified with Charlemagne's nephew that there must at least be some connection with him. Things were left rather up in the air for 200 years until 1814, when R. Jamieson published a volume called *Illustrations of Northern Antiquities*. This contained the story of Childe Rowland and Burd (i.e. maid, lady) Ellen. In this the three sons of King Arthur are playing football when one kicks the ball right over a church. Burd Ellen, their sister, offers to go and fetch it, but never returns from behind the church. The warlock Merlin tells them that because she went widdershins (counter-clockwise) around the church, the king of Elfland took her. Merlin gives strict instructions what must be done to release her. Most importantly, once Fairyland is entered, the rescuer must lop off the head of anyone he meets, and must not eat anything while there. First the eldest goes, and then the middle son, but neither returns. Finally Childe Rowland follows Merlin's advice and is able to defeat the elf king and rescue all the members of his family.

This is a fairly standard fairy story, what is known as an international popular tale, with elements that can be found all over Europe. What links this publication firmly with Shakespeare's snippet is that when the elf king enters the hall in the fairy mound (Joseph Jacobs, whose is the best known version of the story, muddies the water by making this happen in a Dark Tower, which does not feature in the original) he does so with the words:

> With fi, fi fo, and fum!
> I smell the blood of a Christian man!

Poor Tom's words also inspired Robert Browning to write his powerful poem *Childe Roland to the Dark Tower Came* (1855). In this poem Browning tells a story unconnected with any other known Charlemagne story. Instead, like the Italian Renaissance authors (whom he would have known well), he drew as much on Arthurian stories as Charlemagne ones. Childe Roland is alone, on a quest for the Dark Tower, but we do not know why. As he trudges across a bleak, blighted landscape, he tries to comfort himself by remembering past friendships and glories, but each memory of past joy ends in recalled failure and disgrace. Just as the beauties of nature have been warped in the wasteland he passes through, the past glories of the court have been warped and twisted by human corruption. Despite the fact that Browning has used language that is also jarring and contorted to echo the scene, which can make reading the poem difficult, it is well worth the effort. It is Roland himself who tells us the story, as it unfolds. It opens as follows:

> My first thought was, he lied in every word,
> That hoary cripple, with malicious eye
> Askance to watch the workings of his lie
> On mine, and mouth scarce able to afford
> Suppression of the glee, that pursed and scored
> Its edge, at one more victim gained thereby.

But despite his doubts Roland turned aside:

> Into that ominous tract which, all agree,
> Hides the Dark Tower.

Exactly what the Dark Tower is, or why he was the last on the quest to find it, is never explained, only that it has been a long quest, and Roland was so ground down by it he had lost all hope, and was only going on with it because he could think of nothing else to do. Nothing grew in the landscape, except weeds.

> As for the grass, it grew as scant as hair
> In leprosy; thin dry blades pricked the mud
> Which underneath looked kneaded up with blood.

The only living thing in sight was a 'stiff, blind horse' so starved he could not tell if it was alive or dead. He came to a small river, with black water topped with scum:

> Which, while I forded – good saints, how I feared
> To set my foot upon a dead man's cheek,
> Each step, or feel the spear I thrust to seek
> For hollows, tangled in his hair or beard!
> – It may have been a water-rat I speared,
> But, ugh! it sounded like a baby's shriek.

(OPPOSITE)

Robert Browning added a
new chapter to the story of
Roland when he wrote his
poem, *Childe Roland to the
Dark Tower Came*. It is a grim
poem, filled with horrific
lines such as: 'It may have
been a water-rat I speared,
But, ugh! it sounded like a
baby's shriek.'

The landscape on the other side was no better, looking like a churned-up battlefield, littered with what looked like instruments of torture. Eventually, Roland came to some mountains 'mere ugly heights and heaps'.

> Burningly it came on me all at once,
> This was the place! those two hills on the right,
> Crouched like two bulls locked horn in horn in fight.

And he reprimanded himself for being an idiot for nearly missing the signs 'after a life spent training for the sight'.

> What in the midst lay but the Tower itself?
> The round squat turret, blind as the fool's heart,
> Built of brown stone, without a counterpart
> In the whole world.

The last rays of the sunset shot through a cleft in the hills, illuminating the scene. The poem ends with:

> Dauntless the slug-horn to my lips I set,
> And blew. 'Childe Roland to the Dark Tower came.'

For those wondering what on earth a slug-horn might be, Browning had a liking for obscure old words, and he found the word in the pseudo-medieval poetry of Chatterton, used to mean a trumpet. What Browning had not realized was that 'slug-horn' was an old form of the word we now spell slogan (from the pronunciation-unfriendly Gaelic *sluagh-ghairm*, 'battle cry'). Since Roland was so strongly identified with a horn, Oliphant, Browning must have felt this was an appropriate word to use.

Another author fascinated by the idea of the Dark Tower is Stephen King. Although perhaps better known as a horror writer, he has written a series of seven, long genre-mixing speculative fiction novels (plus a number of comic books), to quote King's website, 'inspired in equal parts by Robert Browning's poem, *Childe Roland to the Dark Tower Came*, J. R. R. Tolkien's *The Lord of the Rings*, and Sergio Leone's Spaghetti Western classics'. In these stories, set across different times and spaces, Mid-World's last gunslinger, Roland Deschain, seeks the 'powerful but elusive magical edifice known as The Dark Tower'. He and his companions must save the tower from those trying to destroy it, thereby stabilizing time and space throughout the multiverse.

CHARLEMAGNE'S LONG AFTERLIFE

Charlemagne's Tomb

Many regions have legends of heroes sleeping under mountains until they come again. The best known is probably King Arthur, the once and future king. There are at least two similar legends about Charlemagne, both of German origin. In one, collected by the Brothers Grimm, Charlemagne rests under the Untersberg, a large mountain that straddles what is now the border between Germany and Austria. There he sits in majesty, surrounded by his lords, his long grey beard covering his golden breastplate. Others place him in Odenberg (Odin's Mountain) in central Germany. The pagan name is significant, for Charlemagne fought long and hard to conquer and convert the pagan Saxons. Some say that after Charlemagne had fought and won a particularly long and hard battle, the mountain opened up, giving a place for him and his exhausted warriors to rest. In other versions, the mountain opened to save the emperor and his troops from pursuing enemies. Karl, as he is known to the locals, leaves the mountain at regular intervals; some say every seven years, some say every hundred. As is usual with such stories, a lucky few may find their way into the mountain and to the treasure buried there, but they must be out with their spoil within a quarter of an hour, when the entrance will close for another seven years.

The real body of Charlemagne appears to have had just as restless a time as he does in the legendary accounts. Charlemagne was buried in his royal chapel, now part of Aachen Cathedral, on the day of his death on 28 January 814. In the year 1000, the emperor Otto III is said to have opened the tomb of Charlemagne. We have three accounts of what happened, all written within 50 years of the event. The best known, because it is the most vivid and claims to reproduce an eyewitness account by the count of Lomello, is from the *Novalese Chronicles*. He says that he and Otto entered into the vault where Charlemagne was buried, not lying down as is usual, but seated on his throne as he had been in life. He wore a golden crown and held a sceptre in his gloved hands. The fingernails had grown through the gloves. The two men had entered by breaking through the magnificent canopy of limestone and marble above him. There was a strong smell when they entered. The two men knelt before Charlemagne, doing him homage, and put white clothes on him.

They repaired any damage to the tomb, and cut his fingernails. The body had not decayed, except for the tip of his nose, which Otto had replaced in gold. Otto took away a tooth from the emperor, and then had the tomb sealed.

How far can we trust this account? Lomello was close to Otto, so his words carry some credibility. In the past the idea that Charlemagne had been buried seated on a throne was dismissed as fantasy by historians. But more recent research has shown that there was a tradition going back to late Roman times

A 19th century woodcut, illustrating the opening of Charlemagne's tomb.

The magnificent Roman sarcophagus in which Charlemagne was re-buried by Frederick Barbarossa in 1165. (INTERFOTO / Alamy)

of special Christian burial seated on a throne, as if the corpse was already enjoying the throne of glory that awaited the resurrected body, so it is possible that this was true. There was also a long tradition of preserving bodies by removing the viscera, then coating it inside and out in wax, so it is possible that the body had also lasted the nearly 200 years since it was buried. But it is also possible that this story was told because Otto had intended to have Charlemagne declared a saint, and a body that does not decay was considered one of the signs of sainthood.

The next person to disturb Charlemagne really did have him made a saint. The emperor Frederick I, Barbarossa ('Red-beard'), opened the tomb in 1165. At least, he opened what a vision told him was the tomb, for the location had been lost. Some say that Otto's visit had been considered sacrilegious, and the tomb's location was thus carefully hidden. If it was Charlemagne's tomb, the body had now decayed, for Frederick put the bones in a magnificent Roman sarcophagus (still to be seen in Aachen Cathedral's treasury) originally used, it was claimed, to bury the emperor Augustus. The body was then reburied, but not for long. In 1215 Barbarossa's grandson, Frederick II, opened the

THE TOMB OF ROLAND

The tomb of Roland in the Basilica of St Romain in Blaye has also had a disturbed life, and one that teaches us to treat accounts of such openings with care. King Francis I of France (reigned 1515–47) is said to have wanted to know if Roland had in fact been a giant as some claimed, so when he was in the area he had the supposed tomb of Roland opened. The official account said that the body was exhumed and was found to have been buried in its armour, which, though rusty, was still intact. The king was relieved to find that the great hero had not been a giant, but was in fact no bigger than the king himself. However, another contemporary witness wrote that the tomb was found to contain nothing but a few fragments of bone!

tomb yet again, and this time had the bones placed in magnificent golden reliquaries, one a portrait bust containing part of his skull, another a beautiful chest, adorned with scenes from his life and figures of the paladins. The bones have not remained entirely undisturbed since then, for the reliquary chest has been opened on occasion, including once when the bones were measured to ascertain the height of the great man. And the hunt for his tomb goes on. In 2010 major archaeological work was undertaken to try to locate the original tomb, but with no success.

Sainthood and Politics

As a saint, Charlemagne has also had a mixed afterlife. Charlemagne was canonized in 1165, at a time of low ebb for the papacy. Frederick Barbarossa had deposed one pope and had his own candidate, Pascal III, now considered an anti-pope, declare Charlemagne a saint, a rather dubious basis for sainthood. Nevertheless, the cult of Charlemagne became established, particularly in France. In the 15th century King Louis XI ordered the observation of his feast on pain of death. By the 19th century in France Charlemagne was regarded as the patron saint of schoolchildren. This was because he had set up free schools in his own day, and when universal free education was introduced in the 19th century an

Charlemagne by Gustave Dore.

association was made between the two. Special banquets for schoolchildren on St Charlemagne's Day (28 January, the day he died) lasted until at least the 1960s.

Charlemagne's political influence also lasted long after his death. Although his empire rapidly collapsed, his power as a symbol lived on. By the 10th century, German emperors were having themselves declared or crowned at Aachen. The Holy Roman Empire, which lasted from 1271 until 1806, was consciously modelled on his, and used a crown still often said to have been Charlemagne's, but which seems to date only from the 10th century (and which confusingly exists in several copies). The iron crown of Lombardy, with which he is said to have been crowned king of the Lombards, also still exists and continues to be used in Italy. The French had their own version of Charlemagne's crown, which was destroyed in the French Revolution.

Napoleon went through a phase of being obsessed with Charlemagne, making a visit to Aachen in homage to his great predecessor, and making sure of the good publicity it gave him. When he had himself crowned emperor, he had yet another crown of Charlemagne made, and echoed Charlemagne's own coronation by the pope by making sure the pope was there for him, although he took the crown from the pope's hands at the last minute and crowned himself.

Napoleon does homage before the throne of Charlemagne and the Imperial Crown in Aachen Cathedral by Henri-Paul Motte. (Corbis Images)

The Tomb of Charlemagne and Mythistory in Action

A look at the development of the story of the opening of Charlemagne's tomb gives a fascinating insight into how history (however reliable the account) changes into myth. The rot had already set in by the first half of the 19th century. The influential French writer Chateaubriand described the opening of the tomb as happening in 1450 rather than 1000. No mention is made of Otto; it is the priests who have ordered the opening, and all sorts of vivid detail has been added. Charlemagne is now a skeleton, seated on a golden chair, his sceptre along with his shield in front of him, and a copy of the Gospels written in golden letters in his hands. Joyeuse, in its golden sheath, is at his side. His head, held up by a golden chain, is covered with a shroud over what had once been his face, the shroud held in place by a crown. When someone touched these remains they crumbled into dust.

The story is still mutating. Just a short time on the Internet turns up differing versions. We can see how one writer adds or changes a detail to make the story more gripping. This is copied by someone else, who adds their own changes. Even bigger changes can be made by those with an axe to grind. So we can be told, for instance, that these events took place a mere 200 years ago, and learn that not only was Charlemagne reading the Gospels, but even the exact biblical verse that his finger was pointing at!

Albrecht Dürer's interpretation of Charlemagne's appearance in which he manages to combine the patriarch with the warrior. This imaginary portrait was painted c.1512. (Corbis Images)

In Germany in the 19th century Charlemagne had fallen out of favour as a national symbol as being too French, and attention had focused on more solidly German heroes such as Siegfried. But Hitler had a keen interest in him and issued an edict forbidding anyone to defame the emperor's name. This was a reflection of his ambition to make his Third Reich as powerful and pan-European as Charlemagne's empire had been. A sense of German one-upmanship over the French, who claimed him for their own, is found in the way that the SS division that Hitler set up for Frenchmen to join if they

Charlemagne as the patron saint of schoolchildren, joining them at the feast, which was a regular feature of celebrating his saint's day. From *Le Petit Journal Illustré* 1892. (Bridgeman Art Library)

supported him was called the Charlemagne division. Despite this, a new role was found for Charlemagne after the war. In the new mood of peace and unity that swept Western Europe, Charlemagne was evoked as the Father of Europe (a title he had been given in his lifetime). While some of his eastern realms had admittedly been lost behind the Iron Curtain of communism, six nations that formed the founding countries of what is now the European Union – France, Germany, Italy, the Netherlands, Belgium and Luxembourg – had all once been part of his empire, and Charlemagne found a new role as the patron of the new political union. Every year the winner of the Charlemagne Prize, awarded to someone who has done outstanding work for European unity, is announced in Aachen.

FURTHER READING

History

Einhard and Notker the Stammerer, *Two Lives of Charlemagne* trans. Lewis
  Thorpe (Penguin Classics, 1968). The most important sources we
  have for Charlemagne.

Sypeck, Jeff, *Becoming Charlemagne: Europe, Baghdad, and the Empires of
  A.D. 800* (Harper Perenniel, 2007). A good introduction to life at the
  time, with particular emphasis on the elephant.

Wilson, Derek, *Charlemagne: The Great Adventure* (Hutchinson, 2005).
  An excellent general history and biography, with good coverage of
  later developments.

Fiction Collections

There are a number of 19th- and 20th-century re-tellings of the stories,
  many giving more detail or covering stories not told in this book.
  These are available online, often in several places.

Thomas Bulfinch *Bulfinch's Mythology: Legends of Charlemagne* (1863)
  http://www.gutenberg.org/ebooks/4927

H. A. Guerber, *Legends of the Middle Ages* (1896), chapters 8–10
  http://www.gutenberg.org/ebooks/12455 Ch8-10

E. M. Wilmot-Buxton, *Stories from Old French Romance* (1910)
  https://archive.org/details/storiesfromoldfr00wilm

A. J. Church, *Stories of Charlemagne and the Twelve Peers of France* (1906)
http://www.heritage-history.com/?c=read&author=church&book=charlemag
  ne&story=_front

Andrew Lang, *The Red Book of Romance* (1906), chapters 17–18, 22, 25–27
  http://ebooks.adelaide.edu.au/l/lang/andrew/red_romance_book/
  index.html

James Baldwin, *The Story of Roland* (1911)
  http://archive.org/details/storyroland00hurdgoog

Individual Texts

The Song of Roland. There are numerous translations of *The Song of Roland.*
  Perhaps the best known and most respected is Dorothy L. Sayers'
  1937 translation for Penguin Classics.

Pseudo-Turpin Chronicles. These were originally written in Latin, as *Historia Caroli
  Magni,* although there are medieval translations into other languages.
  There is an online edition of the Latin text with a detailed summary in
  English at http://www.medievalacademy.org/resource/resmgr/maa_books_
  online/smyser_0030.htm#c_ma0030_footnote_nt153.

Roland and Oliver. Most of the material in this chapter is taken from
   William Caxton's 1485 *Lyf of the Most Noble and Crysten Prynce,
   Charles the Grete*, his translation of the extended French version of
   Pseudo-Turpin. The 1880 edition of this is available at
   https://archive.org/details/lyfofnoblecryste00caxtuoft.
   Once you have got used to the spelling, the language is not difficult.
   But be warned, the 19th-century editions have very useful modern
   English summaries in the margins of the stories, which OCR cannot
   cope with without jumbling everything up, so the book needs to be
   read online. The Internet Archive also has Caxton's The *Four Sons of
   Aymon* at https://archive.org/details/rightplesauntno4400caxtuoft
Italian versions. These are widely available in translations, and are also well
   covered by the fiction collections listed above.
Childe Roland. Jacob's version of the Scottish story and Browning's poem
   are widely available online. Stephen King's Roland website is at
   http://www.stephenking.com/darktower/book/
A useful reference book, which gives summaries of many versions
   of the stories, is Willem P. Gerritsen and Anthony G. van Melle,
   A Dictionary of Medieval Heroes (Boydell Press, 1998)